PRAISE FO

MW00425445

Sara Harris has written a poignant tale of life in the Amish west in the pages of Rebekah's Quilt. – Lucia St. Clair Robson, author of RIDE THE WIND

Rebekah's Quilt is targeted at young adult readers, but anyone of any age will enjoy this sweet tale of Rebekah, the protagonist, and the world she inhabits. – Author Hannelore Moore

"Rebekah's Quilt" is a tender love story between two Amish young people that also gives readers a peek into the everyday lives of the Amish during the pioneer era. – InD'Tale Magazine

Sara Harris's Amish novella was a great way to fill an afternoon! She takes us back to the wilds of Indiana territory, leads us through 19th century adventures, and shows us Rebekah's heart when she is faced with the most difficult decision of her young life. When up-with-the-sun chores and a sweet, blossoming romance give way to a mysterious English stranger and the epic blizzard of 1888, the reader not only goes along for the ride, (Harris's adventures NEVER disappoint!) but also feels the heartache, strength, resolve, and faith of these characters. This sweet romance between Rebekah and Joseph is beginning to rival that of Charlotte and Sanderson (of Harris's Everlasting Heart series) in my book! – Ann Swann, author of COPPER LAKE

If you're looking to read a nice clean romance, then Rebekah's Quilt is a great place to start.

Sara Harris weaves a beautiful tale of love and finding one's self in 1888 America. But not just America; we are immersed into the life of an Amish community and a twenty-year-old girl just back from her Rumspringa. – Christine Steendam, author of OWNED BY THE OCEAN

OTHER WORKS BY SARA (BARNARD) HARRIS

A Heart on Hold (An Everlasting Heart, Book 1)
A Heart Broken (An Everlasting Heart, Book 2)
A Heart at Home (An Everlasting Heart, Book 3)
A Heart Forever Wild (An Everlasting Heart, Book 4)

Old Amarillo (Amish Journeys #1)
Desperado
Chunky Sugars
Little Spoon
The Calling
The Bank Robber's Lament

The Saga of Indian Em'ly: The Apache and the Pale Face Soldiers (Book 1)
The Saga of Indian Em'ly: On the Colorado Trail (Book 2)
The Saga of Indian Em'ly: The Orphanage (Book 3)
The Saga of Indian Em'ly: Journey Home (Book 4)

Cheyenne, the Sweetheart of Charlie Company
The Harsh and the Heart: Celebrating the Military

The ABCs of Oklahoma Plants
The ABCs of Texas Plants

The Big Bad Wolf Really Isn't So Big and Bad
Crazy Horse High

Rebekah's Quilt

Rebekah's Keepsakes #1

SARA HARRIS

Copyright ©2019 Sara Harris

Cover illustration copyright © 2019 Elaina Lee/For the Muse Designs

First Edition

Printed and bound in the United States of America. All rights reserved. No part of this book may be reproduced or transmitted in any form or by any means, electronic or mechanical, including photocopying, recording, or by an information storage and retrieval system-except by a reviewer who may quote brief passages in a review to be printed in a magazine, newspaper, or on the Web-without permission in writing from the publisher. For information, please contact Vinspire Publishing, LLC, P.O. Box 1165, Ladson, SC 29456-1165.

With the exception of those identified in Author's note, all characters in this work are purely fictional and have no existence outside the imagination of the author and have no relation whatsoever to anyone bearing the same name or names. They are not even distantly inspired by any individual known or unknown to the author, and all incidents are pure invention.

Print book ISBN: 978-1-7327112-5-9

Published by Vinspire Publishing, LLC

Formatted by Woven Red Author Services, www.WovenRed.ca

To my Dawson, who fears no rooster,
especially not when it's after his little bubba.

PROLOGUE

The Pike, Indian Territory, 1868

"Look Elnora!" Samuel's German accent thickened the English words and gave them a musical feel. He pointed to the vast expanse that spread before them. "That's what the English call The Pike. Many are traveling west on this very road."

Elnora peeked out from the wagon. "So, this is Indiana Territory." Her eyes searched the desolate vastness. She giggled. "I see, Samuel. *Many* are traveling this road."

Samuel swiveled on the driver's seat to look at his wife. He shrugged and a smile played at the corners of his lips. "Perhaps all our fellow travelers have already passed for the day."

"I miss Canada." Heloise Graber kept her voice soft when Elnora turned back toward her. "But not as much as I miss Germany." Heloise patted the back of the baby snuggled down in the cornflower blue quilt Elnora had stitched just for him.

"At only two years of age, your sweet baby Joseph has already crossed an ocean and three countries."

Heloise, the older of the two friends, looked lovingly at her infant son.

Elnora's face fell as her hand fluttered to her still-flat stomach.

Heloise covered Elnora's hand with hers. "Your time to become a mother is coming. God has a special plan for you and Samuel, I can feel it."

Elnora's lower lip trembled. "I must say, at least the weather is more agreeable in Indiana Territory than in Canada. I may pack the extra quilts when we stop to rest." She swiped at a trickle of sweat as it slid down her nose.

"You'll do no such thing!" Heloise placed one long, thin hand on an especially fluffy blue quilt. "It may be a trifle warm but pass those blankets over here. I'll sit on them; they ease the rickety ride."

The women dissolved into a sea of girlish giggles.

"Yours are the softest quilts of anyone else's in the village."

"Take them with you when we swap wagons," Elnora offered her fiery-tressed friend.

Heloise shook her head. The straps on her black head covering flailed about her shoulders. "It's not the same," she insisted. "Part of what makes Elnora Stoll's quilts so soft is the wonderful company that comes along with them."

Samuel's quick yank on the horse reins interrupted Heloise's compliment.

"Lucas, is that what I think it is?" Samuel's voice grew higher as he called to Heloise's husband in the next wagon.

The two women stared at one another, their eyes wide.

"Ja!" Lucas answered. "Ja, it is."

Before Elnora could pull herself up to see the cause of the commotion, Samuel was off the driver's seat. She peeked out to see the menfolk piling out of all the wagons. Lucas was even with Samuel, holding his hat on with one hand and pumping the air with the other. Simon Wagler, Sarah's husband, stumbled as he ran, fumbling with the black braces that looped over his shoulders and held up his britches. On their wagon seat, Sarah nuzzled their infant Elijah, who'd let out a shriek with the sudden stop.

Isaac Raber pulled on his broad-brimmed hat as Jeremiah Knepp, Simeon Odon, and Abraham Yoder pulled their wagons to a halt in a haphazard line. In an instant, all the men of the families who'd come so far together were running toward the remnants of an overturned English wagon.

Pieces of the torn canvas fluttered in a passing breeze and the box itself lay on its side,

Elnora drew a fist to her mouth. "Did it roll off The Pike?"

Blood spatters dotted the ground around the silvery dust that refused to settle around the scene. Splintered wheels hung broken and unmoving from the axels.

Heloise's breath caught in her throat. "No. Indians."

Beyond Samuel, Elnora could make out the remains of a horse just over a small rise. She searched for any sign of the tell-tale arrows she'd heard so much talk of during their journey to Indiana Territory—which was also Indian Territory. She trembled as a prayer of forgiveness for judging those she didn't even know filled her mind.

Heloise's voice was solemn, as if in prayer. "God be with them. All of them."

The men's chatter, broken by the shifting breezes, allowed Elnora only fragments of their hurried conversation.

Lucas's voice was the loudest. "No survivors."

Slowly, the large German-born man trudged back to his wagon without so much as a glance toward Elnora and or his wife.

Without expression, Lucas rummaged only a moment before he pulled the hand-hewn spade from the wagon bed and started back toward Samuel and the others.

Careful not to snag her handmade purple dress on the rough wood, Elnora climbed out of the wagon and made her way to the crash. She didn't speak until she reached her husband, who took the spade from Lucas as he passed.

Not a word was shared between the two men, but it was as though they were of a single mind. Samuel dug the sharp end of the spade into the earth, oblivious to his wife's presence. Spadeful by spadeful, the grave dirt he turned became a small mound at his feet.

He swiped at the trails of sweat that leaked from under his broad-brimmed hat and down his neck. Beneath his arms, circles of moisture had long since stained his favorite blue shirt.

Elnora folded her arms as the memory of their first anniversary, when she'd given him the shirt she'd made for him that matched his eyes, filled her mind. He had pretended not to notice that one sleeve was a little shorter than the other. *Two years have passed since that day, and we're still without a child...*

Finally, she spoke. Her voice was but a meek whisper. "May I tidy them before their burials?"

Samuel turned and revealed the scene of death they'd

encountered more fully.

Elnora's stomach twisted in knots at the sight of the mangled, crimson-streaked arm as it reached lifelessly from behind the overturned wagon. The blackness of death was already visible on the fingertips.

A crumpled bag, obviously store-bought, lay near the bloodied arm that pointed eerily at a rainbow of quilting squares that trailed the barren earth. Elnora dipped and retrieved a bright blue square that would never become a quilt to warm a babe. She rubbed the fabric between her fingers and looked at her husband with watery eyes.

Samuel rested Lucas' spade against his leg and offered a downcast smile to his wife.

Before he could speak, a shrill cry broke the solemn silence.

As out of place as the cry was among the sea of death, Elnora recognized the sound in an instant. "An infant's cry."

She searched the terrain until another wail pierced the air. At once, her gaze fixed on a lone, scrubby bush. Elnora tucked the English quilting square deep into her dress pocket and ran. Her chest heaving, she reached the bush in a moment. Without bothering with her dress or her covering, she dropped to her knees. Instinctively, her hands clawed and searched through the summer leaf litter. The angry wail came again. Finally, something warm brushed her fingertips.

Elnora rose to face the throng of women who had gathered to witness the unfolding miracle. When she turned, the English baby whimpered in her arms.

"It's a girl," Elnora proclaimed.

Sarah Wagler's mouth hung agape as she bounced Elijah absently on her hip, and the other Amish wives and mothers from the wagon train allowed tiny smiles to creep onto their solemn lips. Even the menfolk paused.

Elnora's voice was uncharacteristically robust. "Not a scratch on her! Not a bruise, not a drop of blood."

Heloise, toting wide-eyed Joseph in her arms, stepped forward to get a better look.

Elnora's voice took on the soft shushing of a new mother as she rocked the squirming infant. "Hush now, sweet one. You're safe now."

"You're a natural," Heloise observed. Her eyes twinkled. "Look how she's already calming. She feels safe."

She is safe, Elnora thought as she gazed at the tiny girl. *Safe with me. Safe with us.*

"Come," Heloise whispered. "Get her to the wagon and out of this sun."

Sarah fell into step beside her friend, her blue eyes also transfixed on the English baby. "It's a miracle she wasn't injured...or worse."

"I boiled goat's milk for Katie and Annie," Katherine Knepp cooed as she and the other women joined them. "I have extra. This little one must eat."

Esther Odon nodded. "I have some girl clothes she can have."

Dinah Yoder placed her arm around Esther's shoulders. The memory of Esther's hard labor on the trail which resulted in a stillborn baby girl was a raw one in all the women's minds.

Tears pricked Elnora's eyes. "Danke. Thank you, all."

Day turned quickly to night as the Amish women fawned over the tiny infant who seemed to have dropped straight from heaven, leaving the men to finish the burials by moonlight.

"I understand your wanting to keep her, Elnora." Samuel's patient voice was gentle when he finally returned to the wagon. Gentle and firm. "Especially since the Lord has yet to bless us with children of our own."

Elnora fixed her eyes on the baby who lay asleep in the nest of pillowy quilts in the wagon bed. Usually, Elnora was unable to tear her gaze from the stars in the night sky. They seemed to wink at each other in the blackness, making her think they were simply bright young children, playing gotcha-games in Heaven. Tonight though, Elnora couldn't force herself to look away from the tiny miracle of a girl.

"Gelassenheit," she whispered. "We must trust His divine reasons and timing."

"We simply can't keep her. She is not one of us." Samuel exhaled and swiped his gritty hands on his britches. Exhaustion weighted his words.

"Ja, Samuel, but those she belonged to are now with Our Lord." Elnora sucked in a breath. "Aren't we *all* children of God?"

Her gentle voice wafted with the night breezes.

Samuel rubbed the bridge of his nose. The other men had returned to their families and were already fast asleep in their wagons, evident by several different tones of snoring. He stifled a yawn. "Ah, Elnora. I love you and your compassionate heart. I want so to make you a happy wife."

"You do, Samuel."

The baby stirred and began to squeak. Elnora's voice was tender as she plucked the rooting babe from the nest of blankets. "Come here, Rebekah."

"Oh mein! You've given her a name?"

She smiled and rocked Rebekah to and fro.

Sarah Wagler's shy voice came from somewhere in the near darkness. "Elnora? Samuel? Are you awake?"

"Yes Sarah, we are." Elnora bounced Rebekah in her arms, but the infant's squeaks grew into angry coughs and sputters.

"I heard the baby fussing."

Crimson colored Elnora's cheeks. "I'm sorry to have woken you Sarah—"

Her friend waved a hand and cut her off. "Oh no. You see, the baby sounds hungry." The flickering firelight from the Wagler's dying fire illuminated her timidity. "And Elijah is only six-months-old. So, I thought I might feed her until…"

Worried creases melted from Elnora's face. "Thank you for your kind offer, Sarah. We call her Rebekah. Danke."

Sarah accepted Rebekah gently. She picked her way amid the carefully stacked wares and items back toward her wagon. "Ah, sweet Rebekah," she cooed. "I will share with you the story of your namesake."

"Wake me when you bring her back," Elnora whispered loudly enough for Sarah to hear.

As Sarah and Rebekah retreated to the Wagler wagon, Samuel turned back to his wife. His hazel eyes shone with the tender light of a father. He squatted and scooped both her hands into his. "Elnora, would it be agreeable to you if we keep the child—"

She nodded so that the straps of her covering bounced against her shoulders.

Samuel's face clouded over. "Dear wife, if we keep her safe only until another English wagon happens by?"

With pain cramping her heart, Elnora managed a compliant smile. "That is agreeable, husband."

Her words hung in the air as the song of a night bird laced the momentary silence with hope. "But what should become of Rebekah should we *not* meet another English traveler?"

Samuel's white teeth gleamed above his inky beard. He stood and ran his thumbs along the inside of his black braces. "Elnora, the English are moving west in droves." He extended his hand and helped her to her feet. "The Pike is rumored to be the most traveled route in The United States now. We will meet more English; you'll see."

Elnora couldn't meet his warm and weary gaze and instead nodded at the ground.

"Come, wife, let's go to bed."

With a heavy heart, she complied. When she laid next to her husband, Elnora closed her eyes tighter than she ever had before. Whether it was to hasten sleep or hold in the tears, she couldn't be sure.

Over the remaining two days of their trip, the wagon train of Amish families moving south from Canada only saw each other.

Elnora kept her voice quiet as they approached their final stop. "Not a single wagon filled with English people has passed."

Heloise was much too charmed with Rebekah to be bothered with watching for English wagons. "Such a good-natured baby." Her voice lilted. "At this age, Joseph did nothing but cry."

Elnora cupped Rebekah's silken head in her palm and stroked the blonde wisps above her tiny ears. "And she has so much hair." Elnora's voice took the same tone as Heloise's.

Her friend narrowed her wise, blue eyes. "That means she will be healthy."

"We're home!" Samuel announced. "Wilkommen to Daviess County, Indiana Territory!"

Elnora plopped Rebekah into a quilt-lined basket. Her eyes

welled as Samuel helped her from the wagon. "Oh Samuel, it looks just like Germany!"

He beamed. "So, you are happy then?"

"I am so happy. Danke! What a beautiful place to raise a family. And there is ample wood for your woodworking—"

Elnora gestured wide with one arm toward the thick woods that ringed the clearing. Oak trees that seemed to scratch the floor of heaven stood tall and majestic as their leaves waved in the tender breeze. Shorter, wider trees, blooming in varying shades of snow white and blush pink, punctuated the deep greens and browns of the oaks and lent the entire area a magical feel.

Samuel's large hand came to rest on her shoulder and successfully squelched her gracious spiel.

"Dear wife, I will go in to Montgomery tomorrow to find an English family to take the child. It will be best for everyone if she is with her own kind."

Elnora sucked in a hard breath and willed the sudden fringe of tears not to spill onto her cheeks. She held Samuel's gaze. There, in the hazel eyes she knew so well, she caught a glimpse of the same dull ache she felt beneath her ribs.

She patted her husband's hand as the threat of those selfish tears subsided. "If it is best for Rebekah, then you must do as you will," she agreed.

The tugging on the tender ends of her shattered heart, however, didn't concur.

"What do you suppose Samuel found out in Montgomery?" Sarah's whisper of a voice was edged with curiosity as she rocked both Rebekah and Elijah. The chair was a wedding present to Lucas and Sarah from Samuel and Elnora. Despite the numerous long-distance moves, the precious rocker had held up well as a testament to Samuel's craftsmanship. Not a squeak sounded from the rockers.

Elnora glanced at the midday sun. "He has been gone since before dawn."

No sooner had the words passed her lips than the sound of horse hooves called everyone's attention to the horizon. Samuel was back.

"Here, take Rebekah," Sarah offered knowingly.

When she was situated in the crook of her arm, Rebekah snuggled against Elnora and sighed a tiny baby sigh.

Oh my, she sounds content.

Samuel dismounted in one easy motion. "Elnora, I'm back."

Without any tell-tale sign on his tanned face, he strode to where Elnora sat with Rebekah. His black felt hat seemed to loom over her, threatening to unleash its gloomy news all over the both of them. Samuel squatted down beside her.

Never one to mince words, he spoke plainly. "I met the Englishman who owns the livery in Montgomery. He gave me good news and bad news."

Elnora resisted the urge to look down at the angelic girl in her lap and instead, focused solely on Samuel. "Let us have the good news first."

"I took a wooden wheel and the owner agreed to buy my woodwork."

The sides of her eyes crinkled as her lips thinned into a smile of the most genuine sort. "Ja, that is wonderful, Samuel!"

"After business was discussed, I asked if he knew of any suitable English families looking to take in a baby."

The comfortable sounds of home that had hummed about them faded to silence with Samuel's words.

Elnora's voice came out in a squeak. "What did the shopkeeper say?"

Samuel glanced at the child in his wife's arms. With one large finger, he stroked her tiny cheek. At his touch, Rebekah cooed and began sucking in her sleep. Samuel smiled.

"He said there are no families willing to take in a child. What families there are have all pulled up stakes and headed west. Gold fever, he called it."

Elnora's eyes widened, and she began to sway ever so slightly, dancing with the idea of this perfect baby becoming theirs. Forever.

Samuel's eyes never wavered from Rebekah. "He said if we happened upon an unwanted child, there are places called orphanages where these children are kept."

Elnora stopped swaying.

"These orphanages are filled with unwanted children, thrown away by the English, or whose parents have died. Those children have no one."

Rebekah let out a sweet baby noise and opened her eyes.

"When they get too full of children, as they are now, they put them on orphan trains. They send them from city to city in hopes they will find a home on their own."

Elnora gasped and clutched the orphan child closer to her breast.

Samuel sighed and stood. "Wife, you know what we have to do."

Elnora shook her head infinitesimally. "Oh, Samuel."

He cupped his hands round his mouth. "Families, please come here! I have an announcement." He leaned forward and plucked the baby from Elnora's arms.

When everyone had gathered around the Stolls, Samuel spoke again.

"I would like to introduce you all to our daughter, Rebekah Elnora Stoll." The fatherly glimmer shone again in his eyes.

Simon clapped Samuel on the back. With a teasing note in his voice, he chimed, "If we keep acquiring family members, we will have to call this settlement the Stoll Inn!"

Samuel puffed his chest and proudly displayed his daughter on his arm. "You're right, Simon. This place may become a regular village inn."

Elnora's voice was meek. "Then perhaps we should call our settlement Gasthof."

Samuel's free hand found hers and gave it a squeeze. "How clever, dear wife. Gasthof. The German word for inn. I believe it fits our new home perfectly."

CHAPTER ONE

"Happy birthday, Daughter." Elnora's voice was downy soft in the gray light of dawn. "My precious girl, how does it feel to be twenty-years-old today?"

Rebekah yawned. "Good morning, Ma. I stayed up too late again." She turned toward her mother and tried to will herself to wake. "I simply can't get my stitches straight on my quilt."

Slowly, her eyes opened. The rays from the rising sun peeked into her window and fell across her bed in warm stripes.

The heavy sleepiness disappeared at once. "Oh no!" She sat up, suddenly very awake. "I have to milk Butter."

Elnora's hand came to rest, feather-light, on her shoulder. "Don't fret, child. I milked Butter for you. I wanted you to sleep in on your special day."

Rebekah eased back down into her covers. "Thank you, Ma." A slow grin teased the corners of her mouth. "You know Pa wouldn't be too happy about your dealing with the milk cow in your condition."

Rebekah reached across the bed and patted Elnora's immense belly.

"You let me worry about your Pa." She placed one hand on her round stomach and the other on the small of her back.

Rebekah thought she saw a grimace flicker across her mother's face. She propped herself on an elbow and tilted her head. "Ma, are you all right?"

"Ja. I think your seventh brother or sister will be here earlier than we thought." Elnora glanced at her daughter. "Perhaps he, or she, wants to share birthdays with their big sister."

Rebekah folded her legs over the side of the bed that her father had crafted just for her. "I would love that." She smoothed her golden, waist-length locks. "Mmmm, is that cinnamon I smell?"

Elnora plucked the horsehair brush from the dresser and eased herself down on her daughter's bed. "I thought you would prefer cinnamon cake to chocolate."

Careful to remain still, Rebekah closed her eyes as her mother ran the coarse-bristled brush through her hair. There weren't many snags hidden in it this morning since she had brushed it smooth the night before. "You were right, Ma. Oh, did you happen to check on Cream when you milked Butter?" A flash of worry over her favorite cow's condition caused her brow to furrow.

Her mother placed the brush back on the nightstand. The bedframe creaked as she stood. "Cream was fine. She wasn't very hungry, so I think she will be birthing her first calf soon."

"Spring is my favorite time of the year, especially when it comes early." She flung herself back onto her quilts.

"Oh, my girl, you make my heart glad."

Rebekah fiddled with a lock of her hair. "Is Pa working in the field?"

Elnora pushed both hands against the small of her back and stretched. "Yes, you know your Pa. Trying to get as much done as he can in good weather." She paused. "It's supposed to be a mild rest of the season. But he'll be in this afternoon for your birthday get-together."

"Will the Grabers be coming?" Before the words were fully off her tongue, Rebekah's cheeks began to burn.

Her mother pulled a curtain back and gazed out the window. "Heloise and Lucas will be coming tonight. But not Joseph."

"Oh." Rebekah's musical voice muted. "Why won't he be coming?" She tried to mask the crestfallen note in her voice.

Elnora slid the dresser drawer open and rummaged a moment before holding Rebekah's brightest covering out to her. "Well," she began, "Joseph won't be coming tonight because he is walking up the path to our house right now."

Rebekah's jaw went slack. The sinking feeling in her stomach soared at once and propelled her out of bed.

Her ma's voice fluctuated with girlish twinges as Rebekah rummaged in her dresser. "Shall I tell him you'll be right down?"

"Oh yes, Ma, please," she managed as she plucked a plain, dark-green dress from her modest selection. *Green for spring.*

Elnora waddled from the room and tottered at the top of the stairs.

"Ma, wait!"

With the dress and matching cape flung over her arm, Rebekah dashed to her mother's side. She wrapped her arms around her in a tight embrace and spoke into her shoulder. "I love you, Ma. Thank you for a beautiful start to my birthday!"

Rebekah kept her hands clasped behind her back as she and Joseph, her oldest friend, walked across the meadow. She had walked alongside him too many times to count over the years. First as children, then during Rumspringa, and now as young adults. This morning, though, the air between them was different. Thicker perhaps, more pronounced.

Joseph kicked a clod of dirt. "Your mother's cinnamon cake smelled delicious."

She nodded in agreement but kept her eyes trained on the ground.

If I look at Joseph now, I'll blush and not know why.

"I figured you would have a cinnamon cake. Has she shared her recipe with you yet?" His eyes were upon her, staring. She willed the heat to cool in her cheeks.

If I let him look in my eyes, he will see what I'm feeling. I don't even know what I'm feeling. It's all too strange.

Not trusting her words, Rebekah shook her head and focused on the way his black, square-tipped shoes complimented hers beneath their dark-hued clothing.

Strange and wonderful.

Joseph slid his hands up and down his black britches. "I made you something for your birthday."

An icy knot clunked to the bottom of her stomach. "You did?" Her words came out in a squeak. "Danke."

Having you to share today with is gift enough.

The words were fierce on the tip of her tongue. Rebekah slipped it between her teeth and clenched to keep from spitting them out on the Indiana soil.

I could never say those words to a man. An unmarried man, who also happens to be my friend. My best friend.

"You're awfully quiet today, Rebekah." Joseph shifted his weight. "Don't you even want to know what your gift is?"

She let her gaze meander up the lean, black-clothed frame of her oldest companion. Starting at his black shoes, up the extralong black britches, over the dark-green shirt his mother had sewn just for him, and finally, to his face. The one that had grown so handsome over the years that it often appeared in her thoughts without warning. As an unmarried man, Joseph was still clean shaven. His constant smile readily revealed the deep dimples that made her insides turn to applesauce. "Rebekah?"

She stared into his eyes as deep and blue as the lake on a summer day. Joseph gazed at her in such a way that Rebekah was certain he could see all her heart's deepest secrets.

"Ja?" She admired the way his thick, black hair curled out from under his dark felt, special-occasion hat.

"Do you want to see your gift, or shall I keep it for myself?" His thick brows arched skyward.

The mellow sounds of the lake snapped her out of her trance. "Ja. I would."

I hope my covering is long enough to hide this redness creeping up my neck.

"Good." Joseph meandered over to a nearby tulip tree. He plucked something from beneath the shady branches and started back toward her with two sticks in his hand.

He offered one to her. "Happy birthday, Rebekah. I carved these for us out of a couple of branches that got knocked off the tree there." His voice dropped to a whisper. "*Our* tree."

Freshly carved, the pole's scent reminded Rebekah of fresh honey.

Our tree?

Her heart pounded in her ears as she ran her hand down the smooth wood. "Danke, Joseph."

"Oh, be careful." He reached quickly to dislodge a dainty wooden hook she hadn't noticed before. It was concealed in a special notch in the wood. In his haste, his skin brushed hers.

Rebekah froze. A rash of fire and ice trailed from Joseph's hand on her skin like a shooting star.

Surely our hands have touched over the years? It certainly never felt like that.

Ever mindful of his work, he released the tiny hook from his fingertips. It was attached to the tip of the pole with a single strand of horsehair and dropped like a spider on a strand of web.

"A fishing pole!" Rebekah laughed. "I thought it was only a good-smelling stick!"

"Your *own* fishing pole. Now, all you have to do is find a worm and you can catch our lunch." A mischievous grin dimpled his cheeks.

Her shyness spent at the mention of worms, Rebekah eyed him warily. "I don't know how to fish. Or how to catch a worm."

Joseph's face brightened. "Well then, today's your lucky day, because I am just the man to teach you." He pointed to a patch of damp dirt in the shade of the tulip tree, not too far from the water. "We'll dig here."

He shed his jacket and placed it face down on the grass near the mud patch. "So you don't get your dress dirty," he mumbled.

Careful to avoid his eyes, Rebekah knelt on Joseph's jacket and pushed up her wrist-length sleeves. "Thank you."

"First thing to remember when you're hunting for worms," Joseph instructed, "is to—"

Without waiting for him to finish, Rebekah plunged her hands into the inviting dampness of the earth. The cool mud squished between her fingers and the heavy aroma of the natural world made her heart light.

"That's a good way to start." He chuckled. "Now, simply feel around for worms. They'll try to get away from you, so you got to be quick."

Rebekah moved her hands around in the soggy dirt. "What does a worm feel like?"

"Slimy."

After a few moments, something wriggled against her hand. "Oh, Joseph! Oh! I think I have one."

Rebekah grasped wildly in the spongy ground. As she removed her hands from the muck, the sucking, slurping sound made her crinkle her nose.

"You got a fat one!" Joseph held out her sweet-scented pole. "You want to bait, or me?"

"If you'll hold the hook still, I'll try first."

Their hands touched as she tried again and again to spear the unlucky worm on the carefully crafted hook. The frequent brushings of their skin sent welcome charges from Rebekah's hands, up her arms, and straight into her soul.

The worm, though, wasn't cooperating. The harder she tried to make bait out of him, the harder he tried to escape. Finally, she held him still. With the hook clutched in her fingers, she noticed an intricate little *R* engraved on one side.

"Joseph, what a beautiful *R*." Her soft voice was even more subdued as she admired the tiny print. "That makes this gift even more special."

Her focus lost on the slippery creature, the worm dropped to the safety of the dirt and disappeared.

Joseph's hand, warm and caked with dirt, covered hers. Bits of grass poked off his fingertips as he turned her fingers gently. There, on the other side of the smudged hook, was a perfect little *J*.

Joseph and Rebekah.

"Do you ever think about Rumspringa?" She felt his blue eyes burning into her like hot sapphires. He still hadn't taken his hand off hers, and her knees were as watery as the lake they had yet to draw a fish from.

"Yes. I do." She tilted her chin to look at him. "Thank you for waiting so we could Rumspringa together."

"It was easy to wait those two years." His let his hand fall. An unwelcome, empty coolness replaced what had been warm and soft. "I couldn't let you go off into the English world alone. Or with Elijah."

Rebekah sucked in her cheeks. Elijah had shown no qualms about displaying his feelings for her and had made it well known that he had intended to marry her when their time came to Rumspringa. "I still can't believe he stayed with the English."

She shivered as splinters of fear shot through her body at the mention of the English.

Joseph's normally tender voice turned flat with talk of Elijah. "I can."

Rebekah squinted at him. His body had gone from lanky to rigid. Desperate, her mind wandered to something—anything—to regain the lost moment of gentle comfort they'd shared. "Do you still think of Rumspringa?"

His mouth softened from the hard line it has become. "I think of it often. Fondly."

Thoughts of their time spent with the English during the Amish tradition of Rumspringa flooded her mind. Meant to let the Amish teens get a taste of the English life before deciding to become full-fledged Amish citizens or not, Rumspringa had proven to be more of a terrifying experience for her. Well, terrifying except for the fact she'd shared her Rumspringa experience with Joseph and they'd grown so much closer on a more grown-up level.

He stepped back and squatted at the water's edge. Without a word, he plunged his hands into the lake before he continued. "Do you have any regrets?"

Rebekah replaced her hook on the pole and propped it against the fan of tulip tree branches. "Regrets?"

"About coming back and getting baptized in the Church. Instead of staying with the English."

Rebekah hunkered down next to Joseph and rinsed her hands in the lake. "Not one regret. I couldn't wait to get home." She patted them dry on the grass. "Everyone was so shocked when we showed up early."

She sucked in a breath and basked in the warmth of that golden memory. How wonderful it had been to sleep in her own bed, in her own house, with her own people the night after she and Joseph had hitched a ride back to Gasthof Village with a west-bound family in a Conestoga wagon. "Do you have any regrets?

Joseph dried his hands on the seat of his britches. "Only one, but it isn't important." He picked up both poles and balanced them on his shoulder before turning back to face her. "I think I hear cinnamon cake calling. Shall we try to fish another time?"

Thoughts swirled in her mind like a thunderstorm as she matched her pace to his.

Even with regrets, he still consented to baptism?

She tried out each theory on the walk across the meadow.

What could he regret…coming back early?

Before they reached the house, the smells of baked goods permeated the air.

"Looks like everyone is already here," Joseph mused as they approached the packed Stoll homestead.

He stopped short and waited for Rebekah to catch up.

"Happy birthday, Rebekah. Your birth is definitely worth celebrating."

Something in his voice caused her heartbeat to quicken.

Everything feels so different with Joseph today. Different in a good, grown-up sort of way.

She smoothed imaginary wrinkles from the skirt of her dress.

Joseph placed the poles gently on the ground. "Here, your covering is a bit—" He raised his still slightly grubby hands and leaned in close.

Rebekah ran her tongue over her suddenly-dry lips as he tugged lightly on the white strings. His hands hovered there alongside her neck, close and warm, as his lips cocked into a half-smile only inches from hers. He seemed to be in no hurry to move. "A bit crooked."

His breath was sweet, like honey, as it caressed her cheek. Tingles rushed down her spine as she struggled to make her mouth form words, but her breath hung in her throat.

Joseph didn't speak; he simply stood and stared. The closeness of his fingertips to her neck made her heart pound all the more.

He inhaled slowly and opened his mouth but closed it again. Dropping the strings, Joseph plucked the pair of fishing poles up instead and started off in the direction of the Stoll homestead without looking back.

"Hallo, Rebekah! Hallo, Joseph!" Simon Wagler's chipper voice bounced off the trees that surrounded her home.

Rebekah saw Joseph offer a slight wave to Simon and Sarah, Elijah's parents, as they exited their buggy. She stepped past the line of buggies to catch up.

It looks like everyone from Gasthof Village is here.

The Yoders' fluffy puppy ran through the grass. With each bound, the tiny fur ball would disappear between the blades, only to bounce back up again. The Odons and Rabers sat on the porch visiting, while the Knepps were just pulling in. Joseph stopped to help the Knepp twins, Katie and Annie, out of the buggy.

I wonder if Katie has gotten over her crush on Joseph. Rebekah quickened her step. *It certainly doesn't appear so.*

Katie, in a floor-length gray dress, stood closer to him than Rebekah thought proper in the short walk up to the house. A heat surged in her belly and rippled outward, leaving her insides on a slow burn. Color crept back into her cheeks, but she was powerless to stop it.

"Happy birthday, Rebekah!" Annie Knepp's lively voice melted away the swell of emotions that had surged only moments before. She held out a quart jar tied with ribbon. "Apple butter. I hope you enjoy it."

"Danke, Annie. You remembered my favorite." She slipped her arm through the other girl's and they walked up the steps together. When the front door opened, a barrage of mouth-watering smells washed over them. Rebekah tried to discern each aroma as she greeted her guests amid the buzz of gentle visiting and laughter.

"Good evening, Mrs. Yoder." *Mmm, chicken pot pie, fresh from the oven.*

"Mr. Raber, Mrs. Raber, thank you for coming." *Rhubarb pie, the crust no doubt stuffed with the extra filling.*

"I smell cinnamon cake, our favorite," Annie whispered as the kitchen door opened and a burst of new smells was released.

Rebekah eyed her best friend and pretended to wipe the sides of her mouth.

"Danke! Thank you for coming and for my wonderful gifts," Rebekah called. Annie waved as she, Katie, and their parents climbed into their buggy. They were the last of the guests to leave, besides Joseph, and the sun had long since set. Joseph gave a half-hearted wave from Rebekah's side before he turned his full attention to her.

Did Katie just huff?

"You made a haul. You may well be the most loved girl in Gasthof Village."

Love?

A sparky feeling, like lightning, coursed through her veins at the mention of the word.

He lifted the last bite of rhubarb pie to his mouth. "Stuffed crust, my favorite." He tipped his head back and the morsel disappeared.

Rebekah placed one hand on her horribly full stomach. "Mine too. But if I never eat it again, it will be too soon."

Joseph chuckled. "You know, I wasn't supposed to say anything, but it was everyone's idea to make sure you had twenty gifts on your birthday, since you were turning twenty. How many did you wind up with?"

"Counting yours?"

"Of course."

She pretended to count, even though she already knew the number. "Forty-seven."

His eyes widened. By the light of the oil lamp, they were robin's-egg blue.

"You surely are the most loved girl in the village then."

"The Lord has blessed me by making sure I am a part of a family and village so generous and caring, I have no doubt about that."

Joseph's face broke into a dazzling, dimpled grin.

Like the sun.

In an odd display of forthrightness, words tumbled off her tongue. "But the fishing pole was my favorite."

He held up a packet of cheesecloths, tied up with a black ribbon. "Even more than these…well…things?"

Rebekah snatched them playfully. "Cheesecloths."

Joseph stared down at her. The ghost of a smile lingered on his lips. Slowly, he took a step toward her.

Longing for even the briefest of brushes from his skin against hers, Rebekah forced herself to remain still. She sucked in a deep breath in an attempt to still her thundering heart. His sweet, woodsy scent left her head spinning.

"I'm glad you loved your gift," he whispered. His breath was aromatic, like honey and coffee. "I loved making it for you."

I'm going to melt. Into a twenty-year-old puddle right here on my family room floor.

Ever ladylike, she clasped her sweaty hands behind her back and watched from the corner of her eye as Joseph raised his hand, painfully slowly. He hesitated only a moment beside her cheek. Rebekah longed for the feel of his skin against hers. But the touch never came.

His hand continued past her cheek and touched the brim of his black felt hat. "Goodnight, sweet Rebekah. And happy, happy birthday."

CHAPTER TWO

"Rebekah. Rebekah, wake up." Samuel's voice came from somewhere in the darkness of her bedroom.

She pushed herself onto her elbows in her nest of blankets. "Pa?"

The musical sound of raindrops on the roof left her uncertain as to whether she was awake or simply dreaming. "What's the matter?"

"I'm sorry to wake you, but you have one last birthday gift. Make haste, daughter." Samuel picked his lantern up in the hallway and started toward the stairs.

Rebekah flung her legs over the side of her bed and fumbled for her housedress. Dashing into the chilled darkness, she pulled the hand-me-down garment about her shoulders, not bothering with the armholes. She followed the bouncing light of her father's lantern out the front door and across the yard until she finally caught up to him in the barn.

Quiet bovine breathing filled the dusty expanse.

"What is it, Pa?"

When she reached the far side of the barn, where her father stood smiling, she saw why he had woken her. A tiny calf, solid black and still wet, lay next to her favorite cow, Cream. Its tiny head bobbled as it tried to look around its new world.

"Oh, Pa, Cream's had her calf!"

The tiny animal answered with a weak bleat.

Rebekah and her father shared a quiet chuckle.

Samuel knelt beside the animal and held out the lantern so the ring of light shone on the shiny baby.

"He's a she," he observed. "And *she* needs a name. Would you like to name her?"

She felt her insides turn to mush as she watched in awe as Cream cleaned her baby.

Oh, what it must feel like to be a mother!

She didn't have to ponder long. "We have Butter, and Cream," Rebekah reasoned aloud. "Let's call this one Buttermilk."

"I hear there's a new member of the Stoll family." Joseph's voice was a welcome distraction as she sat in the warmth of the barn, her quilt and needle in hand. "Isn't she a little young to learn quilting, though?"

Rebekah held up a crooked cornflower-blue square. "I need to practice my stitching, but my mind kept wandering to Buttermilk." She plucked a stalk of hay from her quilting bag. "So, I moved out here."

He eyed her work. "I like the color you've chosen. It reminds me of my first quilt."

She nodded. "It was a gift from my Ma when you were born, right?"

Joseph squatted next to Buttermilk and nodded. Cream, who had been munching her breakfast, rolled her big brown eyes back to see what he was doing. She let out a low moo.

"What a pretty girl," he murmured.

Obviously sensing no threat, Cream turned her attention back to her pile of hay as Joseph examined the calf. "Looks like she will have a star."

Happy to delay her project, Rebekah stuffed the needle and inconsistent pattern into her bag. "All I see is black hair."

Joseph gestured to a little swirl on the calf's forehead. Buttermilk kept her velvet eyes trained on him. She exuded innocence.

He rubbed the swirl with his thumb. The baby bovine closed

her eyes. "That hair pattern right there."

"Oh Joseph, it looks like she's smiling."

"She is." His half-grin revealed one dimple. "What a good girl."

He is in his own little world when he is around animals.

A rush of the tingles swept up Rebekah's arms as she watched Joseph in his element. It seemed he and the calf communicated in their own wordless language, both supremely comfortable in the company of the other. Even Cream, who had been more than a little crabby since giving birth, stood idly by as Joseph fawned over her baby.

Joseph is special. For so many reasons—

Rebekah interrupted her own thought before they could continue. "What, um, were you saying about the mark?" Her voice cracked.

"Oh, yes. Well, you see here—this swirl?"

Rebekah fumbled with the knot on the end of one of her covering strings. She resisted the urge to stick it in her mouth like she did as a child.

"I've seen it once or twice before. Always on cows, never bulls."

Rebekah smiled down at the calf. "So, she is special then."

"Very much. The swirl turned white all the times I've seen it and looked like a star. Or a cross."

"Maybe I should have named her Angel." Rebekah's voice was a whisper in the sudden serenity of the church-like atmosphere.

"Hallo, Rebekah. Hallo, Joseph." Samuel strode into the barn with planks of newly shaved wood tucked under his arm. He carried the timber as easily as if he were toting a loaf of bread.

"Hallo, Pa."

Joseph waved. "Mr. Stoll."

"You've been cutting wood, Pa?"

"Ja, an Englishman is here, needing a wheel for his wagen."

A sea of uneasiness rolled in Rebekah's stomach at the mention of the English. Even Joseph stiffened. She rose, her eyes trained on her Pa.

"Pa, an Englishman is here? Now?" She kept her already meek voice at a whisper.

"Ja, the man from Montgomery sent him."

A long shadow appeared on the ground outside the barn. "Lester at the livery claimed the only place to get quality woodwork done was by a feller out here by the name of Stoll. Samuel Stoll."

With a jingle, the stranger stepped into the patch of sun framed by the barn's door. "I'm Peter O'Leary." His voice was deep and coarse. He towered over Samuel, who stood, grinning, next to him.

The sun glinted off the two tinkling silver stars that stuck off the backs of his boots.

"Hallo," Rebekah and Joseph said in unison.

She let her eyes roam over the stranger and made no attempt at subtlety. Tufts of straw-colored hair stuck out from under his black hat, which was cocked over one eye in a decent attempt to cover a vertical scar that ran through his eyebrow. His stormy green eyes stared back at her from his stubbly face and revealed no emotion. He neither smiled nor frowned.

"Does your family await your return in Montgomery?" The sudden sound of Joseph's voice made her jump.

Peter flipped back his duster. Two shining pistols, one held in place on each of his hips by a gleaming black belt, hung there.

"Family?" He spat on the dusty barn floor and shifted his weight, causing the silver stars to clink again. "Ain't got none waitin', least not in Montgomery."

Rebekah cocked an eyebrow before she could help herself.

The manners of the English haven't improved much since Rumspringa.

Samuel turned and studied his wood planks. "How far will you be going on this wheel?" He ran his hand over his thick, black beard. It looked to Rebekah as though he were doing mental calculations, a subject she hadn't excelled in during her school years. She would puzzle over a problem six-days a week, only to come up with a supremely absurd answer. Penmanship had been her niche.

Peter brushed at his nose with one finger. "Well, sir, I'm hopin' to go as far as Philadelphia."

"Ah, ja. Quite a way, then. The wheel I will build you will carry you to Philadelphia."

Peter stared at Rebekah as he spoke to Samuel. "When should I return for it?"

Buttermilk bleated from behind them. Joseph, who had hovered at her elbow since Peter's arrival, turned his attention to the livestock.

"She's hungry," Joseph muttered, mostly to himself. He leaned and grasped Cream's lead rope. "Come on, mama," he urged the sleepy cow. "Let's get you up so your baby can eat."

Peter scratched his nose again. "Mr. Stoll?"

"Hm?" Her pa was already invested in his work on the wheel. Whenever he worked with wood, his mind was so focused that evening could turn to night without him realizing it. "Oh, yes, Peter. Please, make yourself at home. I will have your wheel this afternoon."

"Much obliged." He touched the tip of his hat. "Miss, might you be able to show me to the watering hole?"

The weight of his stare was heavy upon her shoulders, but Rebekah managed a slight nod. "Ja. Excuse me a moment."

Rebekah knelt to gather her quilting supplies. Careful not to look around, she uttered the soft words she knew only Joseph would hear. "Please, komm mit mir."

Joseph's whispers, which were probably mistaken by Peter as simply the blowing of the Indiana breeze through the barn loft, answered her. "Of course. I will come with you."

Rebekah brushed past Peter as she carried her quilting supplies in trembling hands toward the house. Something about the way the strange Englishman looked at her sent a cold drop of fear slivering down her backbone.

After she stowed her kit safely in her quilting room, she allowed herself a quick peek out the window overlooking the yard. There, Peter and Joseph stood without speaking or even looking at one another. The differences between the two men in her yard were like flour and salt. The moon and the sun. *The English and the Amish*.

She adjusted her deep purple cape and gauzy covering and hurried back down the steps. She slowed and drew in a long, deep breath before she stepped back out into the chilly sunshine.

Peter's gaze fell upon her in an instant. "Shall we find that watering hole?"

Rebekah dipped her head in a curt nod. "We have a creek behind the homestead when the rains fall right. Joseph, you were there this morning, weren't you?"

The trio stepped in solemn silence toward the riverbank.

"Yes. We have had good rains." Joseph's words were stiff and formal. "The creek is flowing, and the water should be cold."

He dipped one hand beneath the surface and took a slurp.

Peter imitated him and drank from cupped hands. When he had finished, he wiped his mouth on a bandana he produced from the neck of his shirt. "Much obliged."

Rebekah watched the forced politeness with troubled eyes.

What is it about this Englishman that makes me so uneasy? Immediately sorry for being suspicious, she said a mental prayer.

"You two brother and sister?" Peter perched on a large, flat rock. The question was obviously directed at her.

Unwilling to speak first, she diverted her glance to Joseph as he eyed the contents of Peter's glossy black holsters.

"Well? Joseph?" Peter's voice turned mocking. "Are ya?

"Nay, we are no relation."

Rebekah's heart went from a steady *beat, beat, beat* to a too-quick *thud, thud, thud, thud.*

I hope nobody can hear my heart.

The muscles in her neck and back tightened as the uncomfortable tension from earlier settled over them once more like a death shroud.

"Sweethearts, then?"

Heat flashed within her and burned in her cheeks.

"What about your family?" Joseph countered. "What's in Philadelphia?" His voice was patient and flat, but Rebekah had known him long enough to be able to pick out the little inflections in his tone that could change his entire meaning. She didn't like the turn this watery visit had taken.

"I got some kin back in Philadelphia, so I heard tell. Ain't never met 'em. Intend to, though."

"What are you doing in Indiana Territory if your family is in the east?" Joseph's voice was smooth and serene, as though merely coaxing an unwilling sibling up the steps of the schoolhouse.

Rebekah watched first Joseph, then Peter, with fearful intrigue.

An insulted glint flashed in Peter's emerald eyes. "Why, workin', of course."

"Of course," Joseph echoed. "What kind of work?"

Peter snorted. "Not farmin' like you folks."

He turned, looked off toward the distant north, and sighed. A long, uncomfortable moment passed before Peter spoke again. "I was a lehr boy in a glass factory for a while."

Rebekah was powerless to keep her curiosity at bay. "What's a glass factory?"

The hard planes of Peter's face softened as his green eyes met hers. "Yup. I was only ten when they hired me on. Carryin' all that hot glass's how I got this."

Though the words were almost foreign to her and held no meaning, her uneasy feeling was replaced by genuine interest.

She looked on as the man rolled his right sleeve up and revealed a swirled, raised scar. "A new mold boy was blowing glass beside me. Blew it too full and hot glass flew all over me. Rest of it got my clothes."

Rebekah gasped.

Smiling, Peter ducked to catch her eye. "My arm wasn't so lucky."

Joseph coughed. "What'd you do after?"

"They don't want boys at a glass factory once their hands get too big to pack the glass right," Peter explained as he rolled down his sleeve. He fumbled with the cuff button. "So, after I broke a few pieces, they ran me off."

Joseph shifted his weight and rubbed his chin much the way Samuel had rubbed his beard in the barn earlier. "Ready?" he mouthed to Rebekah.

She nodded infinitesimally. "Perhaps we should get back and check on your wheel."

Peter stretched and offered her a roguish smile. "I knew y'all wasn't related, by the way." Squinting, he looked her up and down in the obvious manner of the English. "You're fair. All the rest of these folks is darker."

Rebekah stared back, curiosity replacing the discomfort. There was something about this Peter O'Leary…

After he adjusted his gun belt, Peter turned to Joseph and offered another faux-tip of his hat. "I 'preciate the conversation."

He strutted past Rebekah. "Tell your pa I had business in Montgomery. I'll be back this evening for my wheel."

"He said he'd be back tonight for the wheel," Rebekah relayed to Samuel as her favorite brother, Jeremiah, passed the bowl of mashed potatoes to each of the younger boys. "Then he got up and left, those little silver things on his heels clinking the whole time."

"It was an odd conversation," Joseph agreed. "He kept referring to family he's never known."

"Let us pray," Samuel announced. The table, which had only moments before buzzed with the jovial sounds of a large and hungry family, quieted.

After the blessing, Elnora spoke. "Perhaps it's best he doesn't return."

Joseph's husky voice sounded harsher than usual. "I agree."

"Me too," Jeremiah told his plate.

Rebekah passed Jeremiah the roasted corn. "He should know better than to make a promise, only to break it."

"Did you finish the wheel, Mr. Stoll?" Joseph's voice was sincere again.

"Ay, I did. I made it my priority." He dipped a cup of water from the bucket on the table before offering Joseph the dipper.

"Samuel loves to make woodworking his priority," Elnora offered in an obvious attempt to change the subject. Her black covering was crisp and spotless despite a smudge of flour below her eye. The hungry buzz returned as bowls, plates, baskets, and dippers were passed to and fro about the table.

Rebekah accepted a bowl of pickled radishes from Jeremiah. After helping herself to a few and passing the bowl on to Joseph, she glanced at the window.

Perhaps Peter is just late.

Unable to let talk of the Englishman end just yet, she piped up once more. "It's still odd he hasn't returned for his wheel."

"That's the trouble with the English," Samuel muttered before filling his mouth with a buttery bite of bread.

As she accepted the basket of fresh bread from Joseph, Rebekah glanced out the window again to see if the Englishman had indeed broken his promise to return.

CHAPTER THREE

A choir of hungry boys congregated around the breakfast table as Rebekah came in from milking Butter. The sun had barely begun to peek over the easternmost horizon, but little tummies were already a-rumble in the Stoll household.

"Have you seen Mama?"

"I haven't seen Mama, have you seen her?"

"I'm hungry. My stomach's growling."

"I thought I smelled flapjacks this morning."

"Someone made flapjacks? Where are they?"

"Who made flapjacks?"

"Can you make us flapjacks, sister?"

Rebekah fielded the flying questions as she set the bucket of fresh milk on the table.

"I'll get the dipper," Jeremiah offered with a gap-toothed grin.

"Happy for a break from the chaotic questioning?"

Jeremiah exhaled a breath he had probably held for quite a while.

Ma must be sleeping late. She always gets tired late in her pregnancies.

Rebekah picked her way through the throng of boys until she reached the kitchen. She passed Jeremiah on his way back in. "I believe flapjacks are the popular choice for breakfast."

"Yep," he agreed. "Today and every day."

Rebekah located the deep wooden mixing bowl, sifter, and

measuring spoons. As she gathered the cooking instruments, she began to sing the rhyme Elnora taught her for remembering the ingredients, so long ago.

Into the sifter dry things go,
To make our flapjacks, ho ho ho.
To four cups of flour sifted fine,
Add four teaspoons baking powder—one at a time.
A whole cup of sugar and two teaspoons salt,
Brings this part
To.
A.
Halt.

She sat the dry mixture aside and wiped up the sprinkling of powder from the countertop. Grabbing the wooden bowl, she continued the rhyme.

Ask your hen for a pair of eggs,
Beat it well with a peg.
Then two cups of milk from the cow.

"Jeremiah," Rebekah called. "Can you bring me the bucket of milk from the table, please?"

A moment later, he appeared with the half-full bucket of fresh milk.

Her eyes widened. "The boys are thirsty this morning, I reckon?"

Jeremiah turned and dashed from the room as though he had somewhere extremely important to be. "Well, it's mostly me, sissy!"

Rebekah shook her head. She added the two cups of milk before continuing the rhyme.

Get your dry mix, add it now.
A half-a cup of shortening, melted thin,
Drizzle it:
In.
In.
In.

While the flapjacks sizzled on the griddle, Rebekah placed the skillet on the woodstove. In it, she placed several thick slices of salt pork.

The boys will like this meal. I will take a plate up to Ma, too.

When Rebekah emerged from the kitchen with the steaming food in hand, she discovered six quivering boys, with forks and knives at the ready, staring at her expectantly. A smile tilted her mouth ever-so-slightly. "Thanks for setting the table, Jeremiah."

Almost as soon as she'd placed the food on their plates, it was inhaled.

After her multitude of brothers were served, Rebekah retrieved the tray she'd wisely reserved for her and Elnora and took to the stairs.

After a light knock on the door with her elbow, she heard her mother's weak voice. "Come in."

"Ma, are you all right?" Rebekah tried to keep the worried tone from coloring her words. She placed the tray of flapjacks, salt pork, and buttermilk on the wooden nightstand Pa carved for her ma as a wedding present. In the sole drawer, crude block letters spelled out *Samuel and Elnora Stoll 1864*. The year they married.

"Thank you, Rebekah. I am a lucky woman to have such a sweet daughter." Elnora's voice strained as she tried to push herself up in the bed.

"But are you all right." Rebekah eased down on the bed to avoid any jostling her mother unnecessarily. She didn't ask the question so much as stated it as if that would assure its truth. "Right? Ma?"

Her mother's lips thinned as she reached for the cup of buttermilk.

Oh no. Her fingers are trembling.

"Here, Ma, I'll get it." Worry creased her brow as she passed the frothy liquid to her.

Elnora took a big sip. "I'm fine. The baby is acting like it wants to come." She lay back onto the pillows. "You may be a big sister again before too long."

As much as she loved babies, especially new ones, Rebekah couldn't feign happiness. Instead, a peppering of questions flew off her tongue. "How do you know the baby is coming? Are you in pain? Is something wrong?"

She flung the words at her mother in much the same manner that Jeremiah flung dirt clods at their little brothers during one of their many "you-can't-hit-me-with-that-dirt-clod-ouch-maybe-you-can" games.

"I began feeling pain early this morning."

Rebekah's eyes widened. Before she could open her mouth, Elnora continued. "Then the bleeding started."

"Oh, Ma, I should fetch Heloise." Rebekah rose from the bed. Her mind was already way ahead of her body.

"No, child." Elnora tried to make her voice firm. It didn't work.

"Why not?"

"We mustn't bother her yet. The pains have stopped and to make the baby come, they must be regular. And hard." It appeared that merely speaking of the process that would bring a baby sapped the very life from her mother. Rebekah patted her pale hand.

"Just tell me what you need, Ma. I'll do it."

Elnora's closed her eyes. "I know you will, Rebekah. Thank you." Her words trailed off in a yawn.

"Rebekah!" a shrill voice shrieked from downstairs. "Help!"

"Ma, I'll be back." She rushed downstairs.

The voice shrilled through the house again. "Rebek-ahhhhhhhh!"

"Oh, my." Rebekah froze at the bottom of the stairs and gaped in horror at the scene before her. Her barefoot, school-aged brothers stood huddled in the corner of the common room at the mercy of Tom the Rooster.

"How did he get in here?" She eyed the notorious rooster as she edged along the far wall. "Where's Jeremiah?"

"We dunno."

The mass of smallish hats and suspenders appeared to quake as Tom dropped his wing and started in their direction. "Rebekah!"

She slipped her apron off. "Hush now."

Cautiously, she slid along the wall like a snake through the grass. "Boys, when I say *go*, I want you all to holler out as loud as you can. Understand?"

Some nodded. Others had their eyes scrunched shut.

Rebekah advanced on the white and silver rooster who, until then, paid her no mind. Then, with a threatening squawk, Tom charged her.

"Now, boys!"

Nobody made a sound.

"I mean *go!*"

All six brothers let out a cacophonous roar. Thankfully, Tom stopped short and turned to face the din, his silly head cocked to one side.

"A-*ha*." Rebekah flung the apron over his scarlet-combed head. She fell to her knees and scooped the whole feathery conglomeration into her arms.

"I'll hold him, boys. You get on to school. Hurry."

The six youngest Stolls scrambled over one another as each tried to be the first out the door and far from the cranky rooster's territory.

"Thanks, sissy!" Thomas, the youngest, called as the lot of them dashed down the road.

"You're welcome!" Rebekah yelled and held the hooded fowl tightly. "Now to turn you out near the barn."

She hurried to the dirt patch outside. Breathless, she gave the rooster-apron package a fling before skipping backward, safely out of the range of angry rooster claws.

A little breathless, she stopped beside a bush and watched as Tom stamped angrily about. His beady eyes glistened as though he knew someone had bested him.

"Gotta get up early in the morning to get one over on me, you silly bird."

The old rooster pointed his beak skyward and let out a disgruntled *cock-a-doodle-doooooooo*.

She covered her mouth and laughed until tears streamed down her face and her sides ached. She doubled over and gasped in a failed attempt to catch her breath.

Rebekah regained her composure as images of Joseph flashed in her mind "Thank goodness nobody, especially Joseph, was here to see that."

No sooner had the strangled words escaped her lips than Tom strutted back into her vision. He looked embarrassed and a sad coo roiled in his throat. Without warning, her giggles were loosed again.

Rebekah sank into a squat and dropped her head into her hands. Instead of attempting to be ladylike, she welcomed the hilarity that overtook her.

"He's a queer animal, but he doesn't seem to enjoy your amusement at his situation."

Rebekah turned her soggy, aching face upward.

Joseph's silhouette stood illuminated against the mid-morning sun. His face wore a dimpled grin as he extended a hand to her.

She accepted it and stood up. "At his situation?"

He arched his black eyebrows and nodded toward the cocky rooster. As the fowl stalked around, the apron strings managed to get caught between his claws. The white fabric trailed behind him like a bad decision. When Rebekah looked at him, he made a little jump, faced the fabric, and called out an irritated *bock-ca*.

The sight was too much. With her hands on her knees, Rebekah gave in to another laughing fit. After a moment, Joseph joined in.

When the mood passed and the throbbing in her sides had gone, she wiped the sweat and tears from her face with the burgundy sleeve of her dusty dress.

"Here, you have a smear." He wiped his thumb across her cheek and left a sizzle in its wake.

Rebekah stood, frozen.

I could live off this moment forever.

Joseph bent to pick a blade of grass.

She blew out the breath she'd been holding in a huff. "Now that's taken care of, time to get busy," she muttered.

"What do we do first?" A freshly-plucked sprig jutted out of his mouth as he waited.

"We?" Rebekah tried to hide the incredulous tone to her words. "I don't know about we, but I have to clean a rooster mess out of the sitting room before starting on lunch and dinner. Then there's laundry, and tending the calf, and—"

Joseph held up his hands in defeat.

She gave him a smug glance and whirled to enter the house.

I hope he follows me.

"I'll get your apron from Tom."

Rebekah stood on the steps and leaned against the banister.

"This I must see."

Mirroring her smug glance, Joseph turned and started toward the feisty rooster.

Tom stood still and clucked soft clucks. Gently, Joseph picked him up and disentangled his feet from the strings.

Rebekah's mouth hung open freely.

Joseph strode toward her, apron extended. "Catchin' flies?"

She accepted it, her mouth still agape.

"How did you—" she began. "No, why didn't the old rooster—"

"If you want to catch a rooster, think like a rooster." Joseph tapped his head.

Rebekah sighed.

He tucked his thumbs under his arms and flapped his makeshift wings. "*Bock-ca.*"

She fought back a smile and shook her head. "Oh, before I forget, when you go home, would you mind asking your ma to stop by when she can? It seems Ma's labor is trying to start."

"When I go home? Who said I was leaving?"

Joseph's stark words gave her pause. She stared into his eyes, which were the same hue as the early spring sky.

Is he joking?

The same gentle smoldering flamed to life in her chest about the time the familiar tingles sparked deep in her stomach.

"Now that the mess is cleaned up, how about some lunch?"

Rebekah brushed her hands on her dress. "Okay, what would you like me to make us?"

Joseph followed her into the kitchen. He reached to the bent nail beside the doorframe and plucked a fresh apron free. After donning it expertly, he held his arms out for her approval. "How does it look?"

Close your mouth, Rebekah, before you really do catch a fly.

"Um, yes. You...um, well, Joseph, you look...you look...handsome."

Handsome in an apron? Rebekah, sheesh!

He retrieved a skillet from under the dry sink. "Well, I meant do I look ready to make lunch. But handsome works, too."

"You're really making lunch. Here? In my house?"

"Yes, I am. Now go check on your ma." With his order delivered, Joseph turned his full attention to the woodstove.

Rebekah crept up the stairs and took extra care to avoid the squeaky one.

Ma should be resting. I don't want to be the one to wake her up.

She eased the door open. There, on the bedside table, was Elnora's tray of untouched breakfast. Rebekah tiptoed across the floor and peered over the bed. Strong and steady breathing came from the nest of handmade quilts that covered the woman she loved most in all the world.

Her pounding heart slowed to a dull thud. "You rest, Ma." Her voice was barely a whisper. "I love you so."

With Elnora's breakfast tray in hand, Rebekah returned to the kitchen. Joseph kneaded something furiously in her wooden bread bowl when she entered.

She slid the tray onto the countertop. "Can I help?"

He glanced over his shoulder. "No, think I've got it."

Rebekah opened her mouth to speak but squeaked instead. Joseph's face was smudged with smears of flour and lard.

Her eyes watered as the same sense of hilarity as that of the rooster incident returned. She bit her lip, but the more she tried to hold her laughter in, the funnier the entire scene became. With an unladylike snort, Rebekah gave in to the throes of a laughing jag once again.

Joseph turned to face her. "What's so funny?"

Sure enough, his entire front, from his forehead to his chest, was spotted with floury globs.

Rebekah held her middle and leaned against the wall. Tears streaked her face and she was powerless to stop laughing.

He touched his face and examined his fingers. With a slow grin, he advanced toward her.

"Oh no you don't, Joseph Graber." Rebekah stepped backward along the wall, but a chair stood between her and the kitchen door. Her sides ached, and her cheeks hurt from smiling. She backed into a corner, completely at his mercy.

"Miss Stoll, you need a smidge here…" He tweaked the end of her nose with one buttery finger. "And a touch there." Joseph dabbed her chin with his other floury hand.

Rebekah flailed her arms and protested through the giggles. The absurdity of the moment made the entire scene even more enjoyable. Joseph's deep, throaty laughs harmonized with hers as they failed to make a delicious lunch.

After a moment, the laughter fizzled away and left a comfortable silence in its stead.

She gazed at his doughy face. Suddenly, he stiffened. "My cinnamon rolls!"

Rebekah watched as he donned Elnora's pot-holders and pulled the delectable pastries from the oven.

How good they will taste after dinner. Rebekah licked her lips. *But then again, anything cinnamon tastes good any time.*

"Joseph Graber, you're a cook? After all these years, I should have known that by now." She dabbed her face with a hanky and feigned annoyance. "What *am* I going to do with you?"

He slid the hanky from her hand and stepped closer. Ever slow, he removed a blotch of flour from below her right eye. He continued to dab long after the flour was gone. "What are you going to do with me, Miss Stoll?"

The vulnerable feeling was back, heavy and hard, in the pit of her stomach. Rebekah gulped. It sounded awfully loud in the sudden quiet.

"Um…"

"Say you'll attend the Spring Festival this weekend."

Phew.

"Of course we're attending." The words tumbled forth much too quickly. "Our families always—"

"Sshh."

Rebekah shut her mouth and tucked her bottom lip between her teeth.

"Say you'll attend the Spring Festival," Joseph repeated, "with me as your escort."

CHAPTER FOUR

Thunder boomed outside Rebekah's window with such intensity, the glass rattled in the frame. Still mostly asleep, she jumped and landed in a heap on the floor. Her waist-length blonde mane twisted in her fall and clung to her face like Peter's bandana had clung to his neck.

With her heart pounding in her chest, Rebekah's sleepy eyes flew wide open to view the world with adrenaline-charged vision. Something was wrong.

Bright flashes of lightning forced her to cover her eyes. Even then, she could feel the brief heat from the striking bolts on her skin.

Fear swelled within her. A torrent of rain hammered violently on her windows, demanding to be let in—or else.

"Halp!" A familiar voice echoed between the squalling sheets of rain. "Somebody. Halp!"

She stopped fighting with her hair and sat as still as a windmill on a breezeless day.

That's Pa's voice.

"Pa?"

In her dash to the window, she stubbed her baby toe on her unadorned dresser. The splintering pain ebbed as the sight unfolding outside met her eyes. "Pa!"

There stood Samuel, pumping water into a bucket so hard

Rebekah feared he would break his arms. Then, he flung the half-full bucket at the monstrous yellow flames that roared skyward from their barn.

"Buttermilk!" The word ripped from her throat with such unanticipated force that her voice went sandpapery.

Her injured foot a distant memory, Rebekah hurtled past her parent's bedroom, where all the little boys were probably cuddled in bed with their mother.

"Jeremiah! The barn—it's on fire!" she yelled into the darkness of the house as she took the stairs two and three at a time.

Her oldest brother's footsteps fell in behind her. "Let's go."

The pair reached the door at the same time. They flung it open so wide that it cracked against the strain of its hinges. Not bothering to turn and close it, they raced toward the barn. Rebekah hadn't bothered to grab a covering and her rain-wet hair streamed out behind her like yellow ribbons from a maypole. It slapped her in the face when the wind whipped from a different direction.

She ground to a halt at the water pump and grabbed Jeremiah by his shoulders.

"You help Pa. I'm going in for the animals."

Jeremiah began pumping ferociously for Samuel who, before that moment, hadn't noticed that his two eldest children had come to his aid.

"Blitzschlag!" Samuel yelled in German. "Lightning struck the barn."

The inside of their cozy barn was ablaze. Piles of the sweet-smelling hay, where Rebekah had hidden from her brothers on lazy fall afternoons, were engulfed by roaring, ravenous flames. The yoke her father had hewn by hand as a boy hung on a blackened overhead beam, charred and smoking. A rafter collapsed, shocking her back to her senses.

Cream and Butter, tied up in their stalls, pulled and reared against the ropes that had now become their enemy. Tiny Buttermilk bleated and mooed helplessly from behind her mother.

Rebekah yanked the knots that tethered Cream and Butter to free them. The eyes of her normally-docile cows were wild and terrified, but she grasped the lead ropes in her hands anyway and turned to lead them out.

She looked at the tiny calf which stood in the stall, frozen in fear. Their eyes met. *I won't leave you.*

Turning her attention back to the task at hand, she sang the flapjack ingredients song loudly, partly to be heard over the roaring flame but mostly to keep both her and the frightened cattle calm.

Another flaming beam snapped and fell behind them. Butter, the milk cow, bellowed and reared. She danced a freakish dance on her hind legs before she jerked free and raced out of the barn and into the heart of the storm.

Rebekah stumbled with the force of Butter's yank but couldn't regain her balance. Before she could secure her hold on Cream's rope, she fell in a sprawling heap in the mud.

Cream. Butter. Buttermilk.

Pushing herself up, she managed to miss being trampled by the cow's frightened hooves that stomped around her.

"Cream!" Her voice was deep and foreign in her ears. "Come *on*." Ever obedient, Cream, although skittish, allowed Rebekah to lead her out of the barn. With eyes rolling back in her head, the more spooked of the cows walked beside her until they reached the house.

As she finished lashing the cow to the front door, a strong pair of hands fell upon her shoulders and turned her around.

"It's over," Samuel yelled. His booming voice was muted by the rain and the fire. He pulled her to his chest in a tight hug. "It's over, girl. It's over."

Rebekah fought against her father's embrace. "Are you trying to convince me of that or yourself?" From over his shoulder, she saw that the fierce fire now consumed the rest of the barn. Angry flames licked skyward from the loft and parts of the roof sagged in an unnatural display.

"It's over," Samuel cried again.

Rebekah stiffened in his arms as a scream tore from her lips. "Buttermilk!"

"The baby's gone."

"No!" Struggling against his iron grasp was futile, but after a moment, she managed to wriggle her way under his elbow.

"Rebekah, stop!" he bellowed. "Stillgestanden!"

She ignored her father's frantic calls as she dashed toward the barn. Jeremiah dove at her from the side, but she dodged his clutches easily, just as she had done for years in their many games of catch-me-if-you-can. Neither he nor any of the Stoll boys had ever been able to catch her and tonight was no exception.

With her eyes and heart trained on the glowing barn, Rebekah ran as she'd never run before. "Buttermilk, I'm coming!"

Her father's breath rasped behind her. Besides Joseph Graber, Samuel was the only one who could catch fleet-footed Rebekah. Thankfully, he was all tired out from fighting the fire. She sped ahead and left him wheezing in the mud outside the barn.

"Rebekah—don't, baby, please." His weak words sounded as far away as Germany as she raced into the inferno.

Ashy timbers that drooped in peculiar places left the roof low and threatening. Getting down on all fours, Rebekah crawled through the smoky mess. "Buttermilk! I'm coming."

Her eyes watered, and her breath came in quick, burning gasps as she kept her mouth as low to the ground as she could. If there was any ounce of cool air to be found, it was along the ground. Still, she pushed onward. After an eternity, her hand came to rest on the soft hide of the silent calf.

Let's get out of here and into some fresh air.

The thought was so strong that the words tingled on her tongue. She would have said them, for her sake and Buttermilk's, but the thought of all the hot air rushing into her open mouth begged her to do otherwise.

She scooped the limp calf up and draped her over her neck before she began to crawl. With her eyes scrunched shut against the sweltering temperature, she felt for the cool mud that ringed the barn.

Any minute now. We will be out of here…any minute now.

Pat after searching pat, only hot ground and embers continued to meet her palms.

Just a little further.

When she thought sure she'd found the way out, her head hit a wall.

She struggled to orientate herself.

I came out of the stall and turned. I should be outside by now— She ceased the thought. *Unless I turned the wrong way.*

A shroud of hopelessness cloaked her. Buttermilk made no sound.

I'm in the back of the barn, not the front.

Paralyzed by fear, the world lurched to a sickening standstill and everything stopped. Everything but the burning.

Rebekah thought she was dreaming when she heard Joseph bring Butter, her wayward milk cow, back to her family homestead. When his voice rose to an hysterical level, her eyelids fluttered.

"Where is she, Samuel? Where is Rebekah?"

Her Pa, though, didn't answer. Somewhere in her sleep-heavy mind, she heard him crying. Jeremiah too. The words "certain death" and "the barn caved in…we can't get in," left an ominous feeling cloaking her bones.

The crackle and sizzle of their warm, safe barn being reduced to charred ash and timber was like a lullaby until a creeping flame licked the bottom of her bare foot. Her eyes flew open and any sense of dreamlike peace was replaced with heavy smoke and hot air. The scream that tore from her throat may well have left a blood trail in its wake.

"Rebekah, keep yelling!"

Something grabbed her dress. "Pull her!"

The something yanked her from the barn into the rain that had changed from a pounding torrent to a soft drizzle.

"She's smoldering—roll her in the mud!" Jeremiah's young voice was panicked.

The sudden coolness was a welcome relief. Maybe this wasn't a dream after all.

Her brother spoke the words that bumbled against each other in her foggy mind. "The calf—she went in after the calf. Is it breathing?"

"Buttermilk." The syllables tangled together on her tongue, or so she thought. Apparently, they came out as a scream.

Joseph's voice was in her ear, soft as clover. "Hush up now. I'm here, Rebekah. Everything will be okay. I'll make it okay." His voice was far away again. "Jeremiah, cake your sister in this mud. Get her cooled down. Samuel, hand me the calf."

Woozy, Rebekah tried to make sense of what was going on around her. It appeared that Joseph's mouth was over Buttermilk's, but that didn't make sense. Then, it looked like her Pa pumped his hands on the baby calf's middle. That didn't make sense, either. The only thing in the world that was right in that moment was the feeling of the chilled muck on her skin.

Immediately before everything went black, Rebekah thought she heard Joseph's voice in her ear again. He whispered something about Buttermilk being all right thanks to her.

"Buttermilk?" Rebekah's voice was lost to the roar of the inferno as she crawled through sagging timbers and shooting flames. The calf was nowhere to be found. Her eyes burned, her skin burned, and even her lungs burned. An ominous snap forced her to look up as the entire roof of the barn crashed down in a splintery ball of fire. She opened her mouth to scream, but the scalding air and smoke filled it first.

"That was a close call."

Rebekah tried to force her eyes to focus, but they wouldn't comply. Her world swam around her as she tried to find Buttermilk. Gingerly, she flexed her fingers. Instead of brushing against charred and burning wood, they met the cool underside of her childhood quilt

I'm not in the barn anymore. I'm in my own bed.

Rebekah's muscles relaxed and ached in unison as she stretched her arms and legs.

"You had a nightmare. I thought it best to wake you." Joseph's smiling voice was an audible beacon from the hellish dream that had almost been her reality.

Someone had moved a chair into her room for him, because the only piece of furniture she possessed that was all her own, besides her bed, was her dresser. Her plain, perfect little dresser.

Rebekah rubbed her gritty eyes. Everything was fuzzy around the edges when she opened them, which gave her entire room a dreamlike appearance. Then, Joseph came into focus. With one long leg propped up on the other, he would have looked as though he was simply enjoying a rest on the porch had it not been for the dark shadows beneath his bloodshot eyes and deep creases in his brow. She drank the sight of him in.

This is the stuff dreams are made of.

"What happened? All I remember is…" Her crackly words trailed off as she tried to disentangle truth from fiction. "All I remember is…mud."

Joseph laced his fingers behind his head and leaned back. His lips spread into a tilted grin. "There was lots of mud there at the end. It seems you got lost in your own barn. Luckily, you were squalling so loud I was able to find you and pull you out."

"Pull me out?"

Elnora waddled in with a tray. "Ah, look who is awake." Her words were breathy, and her hands shook. "Joseph kicked down part of the barn wall to get to you."

Rebekah's brows knitted together above her eyes as she looked at her mother. She rubbed them again.

Joseph smile melted from his face as he rose and took the tray from Elnora's trembling hands. "Here, I'll take care of that, Mrs. Stoll."

"Thank you, Joseph." She steadied herself against the wall. "I think that did me in. I'll be lying down if anyone needs me." Elnora closed her eyes and leaned against the wall.

Joseph deposited Rebekah's tray in her lap. The pair shared a look before he turned back to Elnora. "Can I help you, Mrs. Stoll?"

Beads of sweat stood out against her pasty skin.

What's wrong with Mother?

"Yes, Joseph, you may. Again, thank you." Elnora extended her arm and allowed Joseph to lead her from the room.

I'm so glad Joseph is here. Rebekah licked her lips as her thought was cut short by the scent of cornbread. The smell was powerful enough to bring a growl to her stomach. She tore into her food like a starved dog.

I didn't realize I was so hungry.

The honey cornbread was sweeter than it had ever tasted before and the black coffee, which someone had thoughtfully cooled, swished down her raw throat with blissful ease. Before she started on the thick slice of ham, Joseph returned.

"This pregnancy is draining your Ma. Thank God she's at the end of it."

Rebekah nodded, her mouth too full to speak.

"Do you need anything else?"

She swallowed, a task which had proven better in theory than in action. The chunk of meat almost didn't go down. "Ow!"

Joseph shook his head. "That'll go away in a day or two. Your throat's a little swollen from all the smoke you breathed in."

Rebekah let her eyes fall to her quilt as her hand stroked the odd blue square in the middle absently. She had been about to ask how he knew all this, but before she could, the memories returned in a rush.

She and Joseph had returned earlier than expected from Rumspringa. Before they had the chance to exit the wagon belonging to the English family who'd given them a ride home, both could smell the stench of death that permeated the usually serene Indiana night. The fear in Joseph's eyes was like nothing she'd seen before—or since.

"My family's place." Joseph repeated the words helplessly as they trotted together through the night, which was made darker still by the smoke-thickened air. As they stepped onto the Graber place, a small forest of blackened sticks, still glowing orange at the ends, stood where the barn had once been. Odd black shapes lay smoldering and unmoving.

Samuel's solemn voice came from somewhere behind them. "Joseph, your family is fine. Everyone is alive."

"Pa? Where's my pa?"

Samuel's strong hands came down, one on each of their shoulders. "Lucas collapsed in the barn. Your ma is tending to him now."

In a flash, Joseph had disappeared into the night.

Samuel's arm tightened around his daughter's shoulders. "Welcome home, Rebekah. Not a fine reception, is it?"

"Oh, Pa." She squeezed his middle. "Are the Grabers really all right?"

Samuel held her close and made no move to release his bear hug. "They'll be fine. We will get started on another barn in the morning. I also plan to give him Bacon, our new heifer."

Rebekah bit her lip. "Did they lose a cow to the fire?"

"Ja. They lost them all."

Tears pricked Rebekah's eyes. "Oh, Pa. If only we'd come back a little sooner—"

Samuel cut her off and guided them back toward their buggy. "Gelassenheit, daughter. We must trust the Lord's reasoning and His perfect timing."

Rebekah shook her head and cleared the sad, smoky memories from her tired mind. "Would you mind bringing me my quilting bag?" Her voice was a whisper. "It's in the next room."

With a curt nod, Joseph stepped out of the room only to reappear a moment later with her quilting bag in hand.

She let the corners of her mouth flicker upward. "I suppose I should practice my stitching if I have to lie here."

He plopped the bag at the foot of her bed and helped himself to a pinch of ham. "I still can't believe you ran into a burning barn after a calf."

"You would have done the same thing." Ever unable to take a compliment, she bit her tongue the moment she said it.

"You're right. I would have, had I been around." Eyeing her, Joseph continued. "Rebekah don't bite your tongue. You can speak your mind around me. I ain't made of glass."

He grinned that dazzling grin again, the one that seemed to light up wherever he happened to be. "It's just me, your old friend Joseph." He screwed his face up and stuck out his tongue.

With a giggle, she brought her hand up as a shield against his silly antics and her fingers brushed against a lock of her hair. She froze.

Rebekah's smile faded slowly. "Oh." She fingered the fried ends of her once long, thick mane. The more she felt, the worse off her hair seemed to have fared in the fire. "Oh, Joseph, it must be hideous." A wave of embarrassment threatened to drown her.

He shook his head.

"What you did took courage." He spoke those simple words easily. "You saved a life by almost giving yours. Anyway"—he plucked up her white covering from where it had fallen on the floor—"nobody will know about your hair except you, me, and your folks."

"Courage," she whispered to herself, trying out the word.

"Yep." He stood and sauntered to the window.

She watched how his lanky frame moved with natural ease, like river water flowing over rocks and pebbles. In the soft, muted light of the early morn, he looked especially handsome. He folded his arms and stared out the window, watching the sun rise in the misty morning sky.

"Not many grown men would have been able to do what you did." When he looked at her, she knew he was serious. "Especially for a baby calf."

"I thank God that sweet baby survived."

Joseph's eyes sparkled. "You want to see her?"

She nodded. "Yes. I do." Rebekah ignored the bone-deep weariness that weighed her down like an anvil and started to get out of bed.

Joseph waved both hands at her and skipped sideways toward the door. "No, no, you stay there. I'll be right back."

Thank goodness.

She sank back into her pillow and quilt. Her tense muscles began to twitch and relax again.

I'll leave my quilting 'till later.

The comfortable sounds of her brothers moving up and down the stairs had a lullaby effect. Her eyes fluttered, and exhaustion made her dizzy.

Joseph clomped in a moment later with Buttermilk nestled safely in his strong arms. This handsome man stood holding one of God's most innocent creatures as though he would protect her from the world, should he have to. The sight was so moving that tears sprang up in her still-dry eyes.

"B-b-b-l-l-l-e-e-e-h-h," Buttermilk bleated.

A smile flicked the ends of her mouth upward. "She still doesn't moo."

His voice was a whisper. "I told you she was all right."

"I believed—" Rebekah began. But when she looked at Joseph, his eyes were on Buttermilk, not her. He bounced the baby cow gently in his arms, reminiscent of how a young mother bounced a newborn babe. A scarlet heat crept up her neck.

Without warning, her mind switched gears. "I will miss Bible study at the Yoders today." She had looked forward to the impromptu gathering that had been planned the night before. "Their little puppy gets fluffier all the time."

Buttermilk bleated again.

"Uh-oh, I believe she needs to be outside." Joseph made it to the stairs in three long strides. "Rebekah, I'll be downstairs helping your Pa with breakfast for the young 'uns. He looked like he was having a hard time when I passed him a minute ago."

"Thank you for taking care of me." Her whisper hung in the empty room. Already gone, Joseph didn't hear.

The gentle sounds of everyone going about their business in her childhood home rocked her, in her half-asleep state, much like a favorite rocking chair. She tried to pick out the sounds and guess who would be making them as sleep tugged at her eyelids.

There's Jeremiah…he's bringing in the milk.

That was Thomas…he just ran into the doorframe.

Her heart was light as bits of laughter from her Pa and Joseph floated up the stairs and sleep found her, snug, warm, and safe, in her bed.

Rebekah woke with a start.

Surely I've only been asleep a few minutes.

The sun told a different story. Orange rays entered at an angle through her window and splayed across the bed.

I should be up to my elbows in dinner preparations by now.

A rogue noise sounded from outside. It wasn't one of the comfortable sounds to which she had grown accustomed. It was a pair of chattering voices that didn't belong outside her window. The weighted curtain of sleep lifted as the voices continued and grew louder as the heaviness left her ears.

"Joseph?" she wondered aloud. "Is that Joseph's voice?" It was.

But who is he talking to? Is Peter back for his wheel?

The song of a cardinal drowned out the other voice with its *purty, purty, purty…whoit.*

Rebekah rose and flung her legs over the side of her bed. When her feet touched the floor, the memory of her stubbed baby toe flashed to the front of her mind with white-hot precision. Tears sprang to her eyes and her stomach churned. She hiked her gown up. Sure enough, her tiny toe had taken on a hue of greenish-black. A purple bruise mottled the entire side of her right foot, clean up to her ankle.

She hobbled across the room and peered out the window. Down below stood Joseph, his arms folded as usual, with his trademark stem poking out from between his teeth. When he threw his head back to laugh, she saw whom the other voice belonged to.

It was Katie Knepp.

CHAPTER FIVE

Rebekah limped across her bedroom floor to the simple doorway. A jagged ache gnawed at her heart, blocking out the pain in her discolored foot.

Why is Katie here?

An unfamiliar feeling twanged in her gut.

And why is Joseph talking to her like a beau?

She maneuvered herself out her room and to the stairs with more than a little difficulty. Her stomach lurched as she looked down the steep staircase. Her sweaty grip tightened on the banister. "Well, here goes."

Placing her good foot down first, she leaned on the banister and hopped down the first step.

Whew, that wasn't so bad. Only twelve more to go.

Trying to be as quiet as possible, Rebekah leaned on the bannister and hopped down the rest of the wooden stairs. A thin film of sweat covered her face like a veil as she neared the floor.

Almost there.

As she hopped off the last step, her hands fluttered to her head to straighten her covering. Instead, her fingers brushed her singed mane. "My covering!"

A brief moment of panic brought on with the prospect of ascending and descending the stairs again was interrupted by the thundering of feet. Thomas skipped past, his heart and eyes set on the partially opened front door. Rebekah saw Joseph's back come in and out of view as the door swayed in the breeze.

"Thomas." She swiped at the beads of perspiration that dotted her forehead. "Help!"

Her youngest brother stopped just before he reached the front door. Ever slow, he turned to face her. A hunk of bread, swiped from the kitchen no doubt, protruded from his mouth.

"Hi, th-ithy," he mumbled through the crumbs.

"Thomas, come here please."

He shrugged his tiny shoulders and forced down the bite of stolen bread as he ambled over.

"Hi, sissy," he said more clearly. "Please don't tell 'bout the bread. I was hungry."

She ruffled his hair.

"Can you run upstairs for your favorite sister and bring down my covering? It's in my room."

He wrinkled his nose.

"Please?"

Thomas looked first at her, then at the door before he allowed his big blue eyes to settle back on Rebekah. "You're my favorite sister because you're my *only* sister."

"Thanks a lot."

Thomas sighed. "I guess we do need to cover up that hair. I'll be right back." He started up the stairs, slow as molasses in January. After a minute, he'd ascended three steps.

"Thomas?" Rebekah's voice was gentle.

"Yeah, sissy?"

"Could you please go quickly? For me?"

A gap-toothed grin filled his freckled face. He scratched his nose. "Sure can."

Thomas disappeared up the stairs as the front door creaked a tell-tale warning.

Someone's coming in.

"Oh no."

Rebekah glanced about for a suitable hiding place big enough for a twenty-year-old girl. In her haste, she hadn't even bothered to dress and still wore her nightgown.

Her thoughts came in quick spurts.

Maybe whoever it is won't see me if I don't move.

She sat down on the bottom step and hugged her knees to her chest.

Joseph held open the door and Katie sashayed in. The pair sat down on the seat made for three with their backs to her.

Thank goodness the seat between them is open.

A hot knot formed in her throat.

"So sad about their barn. I heard that you went in and saved their new calf." Katie's sing-song voice trilled in the still air. Rebekah closed her eyes.

"Well, you're half right." Joseph stood and folded his arms. That was a sure sign that he was either completely comfortable or completely nervous.

"It is unfortunate about the barn, but it wasn't me who went in for all the animals." He turned to face Katie and in doing so, faced Rebekah, too. "It was Rebekah."

"Here you go, sissy!" Thomas's voice was a screech as he flew down the stairs. In his haste, he tripped.

Rebekah reached out and made an expert save before Thomas crashed to the ground. She patted her littlest brother and sat him down.

With butterflies flitting wildly in her stomach, she glanced at Joseph to see if he'd witnessed the display.

He stared back, grinning.

Rebekah shoved her headpiece over her sizzled locks. "Thank you, Thomas.".

"You're welcome, sissy," he yelled as he dashed away past Joseph and Katie without so much as a glance in their direction. Rebekah guessed his five-year-old heart and mind were already out the door, off the porch, and playing in the surrounding woods.

Katie turned as Rebekah finished straightening the gauzy white covering. She smoothed her nightgown.

"There she is now. The hero of the day." Joseph stepped to her side. "Rebekah, come sit with Katie and me."

He took her hand and led her across the living room as she tried to hide her limp.

She spoke first and tried to keep her voice even despite the sour taste in her mouth. "Katie, thank you for my pouch of quilting squares." Despite their mutual object of affection, Rebekah was serious in her appreciation. "Did you piece them together yourself?"

Katie nodded. "I did. 'Fraid I'm not much of a quilter, so they're a little uneven. Nothing like your ma's."

Rebekah shifted her weight on the seat. "My squares aren't anything like Ma's, either."

She shifted her attention to Joseph. "How was breakfast?"

"Well, everyone was fed. If there were any complaints, I didn't hear them." He brushed the end of his nose with his thumb. "But then again, I made it a point not to listen."

Katie giggled.

"I'm surprised to find you two here." Rebekah didn't mean for her voice to come out as harsh as it did. "What I mean is," she sputtered to clarify, "I thought everyone was going to gather at the Yoders today."

Joseph extended his hand to her. "There was a change of plans."

She accepted it, stood, and hobbled toward the door. Needles of pain pricked her foot. She bit her tongue and squeezed Joseph's hand.

He pushed the door open and revealed the busy scurrying of all the Gasthof Village families.

Mr. Yoder and Mr. Knepp were pushing up the new wooden frame of their barn as Mr. Raber and Mr. Odon steadied them from the top. They called out orders and requests in German, giving the clearing around their house the old-world feel that Rebekah knew only from her mother's stories.

Her Pa, Joseph's Pa, and Simon Wagler unloaded goods from the row of parked wagons. Piles of hay, animal feed, and tack were stacked about in an orderly fashion.

Tears welled in her eyes. "Everyone came here?"

Joseph nodded.

"Instead of going to services?" Her hand fluttered to her chest and grasped at her nightgown.

His voice was soft and warm. "Sometimes, the best way to love God is through action, not through talking."

"Anyway, where else would we go?" Joseph's tender voice was a whisper through her covering.

Katie coughed.

As he turned back toward the sitting room, he bumped

Rebekah's tender toe.

Stars filled her vision and doubled her over.

Worried creases pinched his eyebrows together. "What's this?" His sapphire-blue eyes searched her face with such scrutiny that a sudden sense of self-consciousness forced her to hug her arms to her chest.

Joseph's breath was warm on her ear. "Why can't you walk?"

You're not alone, Rebekah. You're on display.

Rebekah's gaze flickered to the ever-silent Katie. "I, well, I sort of—"

The contender for Joseph's affections sat stock still, her hands clasped neatly in her lap as she took in the scene unfolding before her.

The burgundy color of Katie's dress is remarkably similar to one that is folded in my own drawer upstairs.

Joseph's fingers fell lightly on the crook of her arm as she wrung her hands at her waist. The brief, deliberate touch brought knots to her stomach. Rebekah let her sheepish gaze meet his and the world around them melted down, down, down until nothing remained except the angular, dimpled face of the man who had stolen her heart.

In that moment, only the two of them remained, their eyes locked together and his fingers still resting on her arm. She drew in a shuddering breath as Joseph wet his full lips with the tip of his tongue.

The overwhelming urge to seize the unanticipated moment and pull him close surged through her and left her feeling weak inside. And guilty.

Stop it, Rebekah.

She swallowed hard.

Save these urges for your husband. When you're married. Not for brief moments such as these.

"Rebekah." His voice bubbled into her daydream.

"Hmmm?"

"What did you do to your leg?"

"Oh, that." Rebekah lifted them hem of her gown and revealed her bare, swollen foot. "It's nothing."

Joseph's blue eyes widened.

She shrugged. "When I heard something outside last night, I

dashed to the window. I realized later my foot must've caught the dresser."

"Rebekah, why didn't you tell me?" His voice was hard. "You shouldn't walk on that."

As the front door swung open again, he bent and swooped her into his arms. Lean, muscled arms from all the heaving and hauling that came with being an Amish man.

Katie's mouth formed a perfect 'o.' "Why, that's not fittin' at all."

The heat that burned in Rebekah's neck crept up to color her face, but the warmth from Joseph's closeness and his fresh, woodsy scent made it hard to focus on anything else, even embarrassment.

The door slammed shut as Heloise Graber stopped inside the house. A tiny gasp escaped her lips as she stared at her only son as he stood in the middle of the room with the delicate Stoll daughter wrapped in his embrace.

"What's all this?"

"I was about to ask the same question." The hurt in Katie's voice was almost tangible. "My ma says such behavior should be saved for marriage and no man should—" Her eyes flickered to Rebekah. "No man should go around touching just any old girl."

Heloise raised a hand. "Katie, let Joseph speak." She shifted her patient gaze to her son. "Joseph? You must know how this looks."

He gave Rebekah a tiny squeeze. The embarrassment made her insides quake. "I understand how this might look inappropriate," he began. "But I also know how *this* looks. Rebekah, show my mother your foot."

With a tiny kick, she revealed her mottled and swollen ankle to the anxious onlookers.

"You don't need to walk on that foot, Rebekah." Joseph's voice was stern as he turned his attention back to her. "I'm taking you up to bed."

Happy crinkles creased the corners of Heloise's eyes. "I knew there would be an explanation. Rest well Rebekah and do as Joseph tells you. He's good at doctor'n."

Rebekah soaked up his closeness and blotted out the rest of the room. She inhaled and closed her eyes. His scent was woodsy, like he'd traipsed through a pine forest.

"And you're gonna rest." His breezy voice, meant to reassure, stoked the gentle heat that smoldered in her chest.

She watched Joseph's angular jaw flex as he ascended the stairs. Katie's high-pitched words, like "inappropriate" and "shameless" caught her attention, but a genial laugh from Heloise quelled any anxiety before it had the chance to bloom.

"I'll take care of things. You just get well." Joseph laid the cool rag on her puffy foot. The purple mottling now creeped up her leg, and her entire foot was a deep-green hue.

"That toe is broke," Joseph observed. "I'm sure Ma'll be in here to check on you later. After she checks on Elnora, I reckon."

Rebekah spread her hands over her quilt. A sudden tiredness tugged at her eyelids. "I'll close my eyes a minute, then get up to start dinner." A yawn interrupted her planning.

"Dinner, pshaw." Joseph shook his head and waved both hands as if to dismiss her. "I'll take care of dinner."

"Are you sure?"

"You do trust me, don't you?"

A note in his voice gave her pause. "Trust you?"

He offered her a sly wink that transformed her insides into hopeless mush. "You *can* trust me, Rebekah."

Surely he doesn't know, er, think, I went downstairs to check up on him and Katie?

Her mushy insides quivered. She hoped the flush that flamed in her face wasn't as visible as it felt.

"Do you?"

She nodded. What she couldn't trust was her own voice.

"So, I trust you won't wander down the stairs for the rest of the day?"

"I won't."

He gestured to her nightstand. "Your quilting bag is sitting right there if you get the urge to stitch." The end of his mouth tilted upward. Rebekah liked the way the corners of his eyes crinkled when he smiled. He was even more alluring than usual.

"I'll be back to check on you later." He reached for the handle of the closed door. Before he could pull it open, it flung inward and whacked him squarely on the nose.

Heloise's thickly accented voice rang through the air. "Whoopsie! Sorry, son."

With her green eyes a-sparkle, she breezed into the room. "Rebekah, I see you made it upstairs." The elder Graber flounced across the room with a youthful gaiety that belied her forty years.

Rebekah flickered her gaze to Joseph.

"How's everyone doing outside, Ma?"

"Ah, everyone is fine, fine." There was a dismissive quality to her voice. "I come to see the hero of the day."

She perched on the foot of Rebekah's bed like a plump bird. Her smile was wide and bright beneath the fiery locks that peeked out from her black covering.

"The men are replacing the barn, Rebekah," she reported. "And all the women brought supplies and food. Oh!"

Heloise hopped up and danced back across the room.

Joseph and Rebekah inhaled in unison when she reappeared with a full basket of home baked goods.

"Mmm, I smell apple strudel!" Rebekah licked her lips.

Heloise plopped the basket on the bed and folded her arms as Rebekah began to unpack it with zest.

His eyes bright, Joseph looked on from the doorway.

"Apple strudel," she confirmed and took a big whiff of the first plate before she placed it to the side. "Apple butter. A loaf of buttermilk bread. Noodles and chow chow. And, oh my goodness, a rhubarb pie! Thank you, Heloise."

"Don't sank me, sank Katie." Heloise's German accent was as thick as the creamy strudel frosting. "'Twas her idea to fix you a basket."

"I will thank her." Rebekah's voice was muted and humble. "Oh, what's this?"

Slowly, she drew the heavy object from the bottom of the basket. "Sewing shears?"

Confused, she looked at Heloise.

The stout woman's face softened. Laugh lines from years of smiling and happy laughter smoothed over her high cheek bones. "For your hair, my love."

Rebekah stared at the gleaming shears a moment before

unwelcome tears filled her eyes.

Joseph removed his hat and tossed it onto Rebekah's bed. He slicked back his own thick, dark hair. "Cut it to look like mine, Ma."

A wave of emotion surged from the depths of Rebekah's soul. But instead of coming in the form of tears, it came out as a belly laugh.

Her companions joined in the guffaw until the three of them were in stitches. A low moan from the hallway interrupted their jovial jag.

"Oww," the voice moaned. "Help, please!"

"Elnora."

"Ma."

Rebekah and Heloise's eyes met, and each spoke at the same time. "I'm coming!"

Heloise reached the door as Rebekah struggled to untangle her legs from her nest of blankets. "Hold on Ma, I'm coming."

"Stay dere!" Heloise instructed from the hallway. "Yosef, make sure she stays put and eats."

"Yes, ma'am." Joseph pushed the door shut.

"You heard the lady." Gently, he tucked the quilt back around her. "It's time for the baby to come, is all."

Rebekah nodded, but the image of her mother's gaunt face was a hard one to shake from her mind.

Ma. Please be okay.

Joseph sat on the edge of the bed and studied the food. Finally, he selected the first plate. "Let's eat some of this strudel first. My ma's good at takin' care of folks, so we can relax."

Rebekah eased back against the pillow, but her spine stayed stiff in case she should need to jump up and assist. "I know she is. And she's the best at bringing babies."

They had finished the strudel and were opening the apple butter when the door creaked to reveal Heloise's corpulent frame.

"Rebekah, darling, you will have a baby sibling soon. Your Ma's been laboring for some time." She rubbed her eyes. "I will help bring baby."

Rebekah sighed as Heloise sat on the wooden chair next to her.

Thank you, God.

Somehow, the apple butter smelled even sweeter now.

"Having the village midwife to attend to her is a lot better than the eldest daughter. You soothed my fears, Heloise."

Joseph tilted his chin. "Told you so."

"Heloise." Elnora's voice, filled with pain, echoed in the silent hallway. "Helois-s-s-s-e!"

Heloise pushed herself out of the chair and charged through the door in one discombobulated motion. At once, Rebekah saw that something was off.

"Oh." Heloise's voice was an excited huff as she bounced out the door, her feet all a tangle.

"Joseph, she can't get her balance."

"Ma!" Joseph dashed after her.

But he was too late. The sickening thunk-thunk-thunk as Heloise tumbled down the stairs had already come to a stop.

CHAPTER SIX

Rebekah woke with a crick in her neck. Carefully, she pulled her head up from the uneven quilt that still lay tucked underneath her.

She tried to push up on the arm that had moments before been bent beneath her.

This arm's as useless as a hunk of dead wood.

Her arm pulsed back to life as the blood rushed into it.

I must have fallen asleep. Still, she was sleep-dumb from exhaustion. The moonlight streamed in through the window and cast a pale, silvery sheen on the floor.

Rebekah flexed her arm. She winced from the pain that stabbed in her neck and shoulder.

The sounds of the men who still worked outside met her ears. Her father's jovial voice rang out above the rest as he joshed with Lucas, Simon, and the rest of the Gasthof Village men who had come to lend their strong hands. She lifted a hand to her stiff neck.

Rebekah heard Mr. Yoder's voice saying something in German about the women having left for the night. Someone else answered that was unfortunate because he could use a slice of stuffed crust apple pie right about now. Their genial laughter wafted in through her open window like soft, melodic breezes.

She rubbed her tense neck muscles so hard, her fingers tingled as she tried to think back to when exactly she fell asleep.

Was it after Joseph and Lucas splinted Heloise's broken leg and took her home?

No, she remembered the relief she felt when she learned that Heloise's only injury from her fall had been a broken leg.

After a moment of rubbing, a loud pop from an odd place between her shoulder and neck brought her momentary relief. She released the breath she hadn't realized she was holding. Moving her tingling arm gingerly, she shifted her position in the bed.

Was it after Mrs. Yoder came up to check on Ma's progress?

No, she remembered Mrs. Yoder's soft voice telling her that her mother's labor was progressing slowly. She had claimed to be positive that it would be at least a few days longer before the baby would make an appearance.

Gently, Rebekah picked up the quilt piece and examined it. Her throbbing arm made it hang lopsided before her. She'd worked on it for what seemed like forever, but there was still so much that needed to be completed before it was finished.

She glanced into the bag. It contained more than enough squares to finish the quilt. Then, she looked back to her handiwork. It simply didn't *look* the way a quilt was supposed to look. Especially not like Elnora's at this stage in the process.

The stitches were crooked. They made Katie's look closer to perfect than hers had ever been. Her morning star pattern, which was constructed from pieces of dresses she had saved from her younger days, was off-center and uneven. Not even her squares were uniform. Try as she might, she hadn't been able to cut any two squares the same size. Even worse, the fabric was rumpled from constantly being shoved into her bag.

"At least I've finally gotten the knack of double-stitching so that my pieces actually stay together," she muttered.

Despite everything, the result was little more than a sad excuse for a quilt-in-progress. Rebekah yawned in the thick, damp air. She leaned sideways and placed her project on the bedside dresser.

"Help, please," a breathy voice managed from the hallway.

"Ma?"

She slid her legs over the side of her bed and eased them down until her feet met the hardwood floor. Her father had laid this floor expertly in only a few days, or so she'd heard tale.

Shards of pain sparked up her leg and her stomach lurched. She choked on the yell that strangled in her throat as the rest of her body joined her feet on the floor. Tears blurred her wobbly vision.

A strained groan came from the direction of her parent's room.

Rebekah shook the foggy stars from her head.

Standing up isn't an option. She flexed her multi-hued ankle as she sat on the chilled floor that had moments before been her ally. *Nope, certainly not an option.*

A series of pants echoed in the dark hallway.

"I'm coming, Ma."

Ignoring the seeping dankness, she stretched out on the floor in her thin nightgown and pulled herself along the smooth boards with her hands. She slithered to the doorway like a snake through the grass.

Rebekah managed to navigate around the doorframe only to knock her head on something stationary that shouldn't be there. "Ow!"

Her mother's labored breathing drew Rebekah's attention from her own sudden pain.

"Rebekah," she rasped. She seemed completely oblivious to the fact that her daughter's head had just met her nose. Hard.

"Ma, are you okay?" The absurdity of that question filled the air. Of course her pregnant mother, lying here alone in the early morning darkness, was not okay.

"The baby."

She didn't wait for her to finish. She scurried to her mother's feet and paled at what she saw.

By muted moonlight, it was obvious that the dark pool beneath her mother was blood.

"Mrs. Yoder said the baby wouldn't be coming for a while," Rebekah stammered. She chewed the inside of her lip as the sea of churning thoughts attempted to push a coherent solution to this predicament into the forefront of her mind. It didn't work.

Clear fluid puddled around her mother in stark contrast to the crimson stains. "Something's wrong." Tension broke her words in unnatural places. "With the baby—something's wrong."

Helpless tears sprang into Rebekah's eyes without warning. "What, Ma. Tell me what's wrong." She swiped at her face with the back of her hand. "Tell me what's wrong and I'll fix it."

A grunt from Elnora gave her pause. "I have to push."

She fumbled with her mother's nightgown. "You push if you need—" Rebekah sucked in a hard breath. "Ma, I see feet."

Elnora stopped panting. "Feet?" She shook her head in tiny shakes. "Oh, Rebekah, no. No!"

"What do I do?" Hysteria rose in her throat and pinged the ends of her words.

"Turn him. Turn the baby."

The sea of thoughts began to churn again in Rebekah's mind. This time, they were vicious and wild.

"Ma," she began. Icy fingers of fear clenched tightly at her throat. A very real pain seared there, just beneath her chin. "I don't know what to do."

"Dear Father," Elnora prayed, oblivious to Rebekah's plight. "Please turn the baby or he'll die."

Rebekah placed her hands alongside the tense bulge on Elnora's stomach. "Please Father, help me save my little brother or sister."

She closed her eyes and tried to visualize how he or she was laying. Her eyes still closed, she began to sing.

"Dein heilig statt hond sie zerstört." She crooned the ancient song, penned by early Anabaptist martyr Leonhard Schiemer, in Pennsylvania Dutch. She drew out each word of the hymn as long as the note would allow and gave her song a peaceful, chanting feel. Rebekah lowered her face nearer to her mother's belly. Singing in a steady and even tone, she continued. "Dein Altar umgegraben."

She pressed against the bulge with a firm hand and felt the fluttering movements of her tiny sibling.

"Oh," Elnora cried. "He's moving!" Sobs overtook her words. Rebekah noticed a trembling in her mother's knees that wasn't there before.

Sure enough, under the pressure of her hand, the baby was turning.

Elnora whimpered and shoved her hand into her mouth. Rebekah noticed a trickle of blood drip down her mother's wrist.

Rebekah felt a fullness settle into her mother's lower abdomen.

"Thank you, Father," she prayed. Streams of sweat stung her

eyes and glued her hair to her forehead. The solemn hymn still crept from her lips. "Dazu auch deine Knecht ermördt."

Beneath her hands, her mother's belly tightened, and Elnora began to push.

Her mother screeched.

"The head!" Rebekah announced. "It's a head."

Her mother's mind was elsewhere, far removed from her daughter as she worked hard to bring her baby into the world. She was silent after the scream, her eyes shut tight.

The front door slammed, and booted footsteps pounded across the bottom floor, then up the stairs. Rebekah held her sibling's fuzzy, black-topped head as the baby began to rotate again. Then it stopped.

Joseph's head appeared above the staircase.

"What do you want me to do?" His voice sounded as frenzied as she felt.

"It's stuck!" Elnora's words were tinged in fear.

Rebekah leaned in to investigate. "Joseph! I need the shears!"

Joseph stumbled up the stairs, tripped, and slid into Rebekah's bedroom. A moment later, he scuttled out with shears in hand. "Here!"

She took them and snipped the cord that had become entangled around the baby's neck. The rest of his robust body slid out easily.

"I need something to wrap him in."

Joseph disappeared and returned a moment later with her partially-completed quilt. Without a second thought, she swaddled the baby and rubbed his back with her palm.

"Go tell Pa we've got a little Benjamin," Rebekah ordered, not thinking to be polite.

"Benjamin, right," Joseph repeated as he hurried toward the stairs. "I got back just in time."

Baby Benjamin loosed a piercing cry into the darkness.

"Thank you again, God. You were with all of us from start to finish."

She cooed and rocked the angry baby. "Ma, he's a fine boy. Baby Benjamin. We'll call him Beanie."

Silence.

"Ma?"

Samuel and Joseph emerged from the blackness. "Ma won't answer me!" Her voice wavered, helpless, in the darkness.

Samuel was at Elnora's head in an instant, cooing and rubbing her forehead.

Joseph stood on the top stair and, for the first time Rebekah could remember, he looked awkward and out of place. He wrung his hands at his waist and, with his gaze darting about, seemed unable to focus on anything.

In the sudden silence, Rebekah noticed that all the happy sounds that had filled her home moments before suddenly ceased. All that remained were tiny, sweet sucking noises as Beanie ate his fist and her father's muffled pleas of as he begged her mother to live. Beanie screeched again, his cry shattering the grave moment.

Samuel's head snapped up. His long black beard swept over the end of Elnora's nose.

"My new baby son." His voice broke.

Rebekah could only point as her mother brushed her nose with one weak hand.

Elnora groaned and shifted on the unforgiving floor.

Samuel cradled his wife's head in his hands. Tears glistened on his cheeks and hung from his inky beard like early morning dewdrops in a cobweb. "Thank you, Father." The words formed quietly on his lips.

Beanie screeched again.

"Here, mama." Samuel scooped his wife easily into his muscled, dusty arms. "Let me get you into the bed."

"What's goin' on—" Little Isaac's voice was heavy with sleep.

"—out here?" Abram, his twin, finished. The pair yawned at the same time.

Rebekah snapped into big sister mode. "Nothing for eight-year-old eyes to see."

"Then what's that on the floor?"

"Yeah, Rebekah, what's that on the floor?"

As the sleep faded from their eyes, the unending stream of questions began.

"And what'cha holding?"

"An' what was that noise earlier? It sounded like a bawlin' calf."

Joseph placed a hand on both boys' shoulders. His singsong

voice was lullaby low as he led them back to their beds.

"Go on back to sleep and dream of all the surprises tomorrow has in store for you."

Rebekah winced at the word *surprise*, which was not the optimal way to lure little eight-year-old brothers back to bed.

Abram and Isaac rubbed their eyes. "Surprises?"

Joseph didn't falter over his poor choice of words. "Each day is a gift from the Lord. So, it stands to reason that within each gift, there is a surprise."

The boys looked first at each other, then at Joseph. "Really?"

Rebekah shook her head as the trio disappeared into the bedroom. Beanie squirmed in her arms and coughed. Obviously hungry, he began to sputter and fuss. She bounced him up and down.

Joseph emerged a moment later. He wiped make-believe sweat from his brow. "Maybe I shouldn't have said surprise."

"How'd you get them to go sleep?" She held the bundle of boy toward Joseph. He held him expertly in one arm and extended the other to her.

Rebekah took it and pulled herself to her feet. She tested the weight on her bad foot. Pins pricked up her leg and she grunted.

"Well," he started, "I simply explained that in each day, or each gift from the Lord, is a surprise. It's up to us to find our own special surprise from Him each day."

His eyes shone like onyx as he stared into her face. In his haste to be of assistance, he'd lost his hat. Locks of ebony hair stuck out in all directions and a few were plastered to his forehead. Rebekah's stomach lightened with the beats of butterfly wings. Silvery moon rays streamed through the hall window and illuminated their linked arms.

For one moment, one brief, illogical moment, Rebekah allowed herself to pretend that Joseph was telling her how he'd gotten their own sons to sleep, not her little brothers. Deep, inner warmth pulsed through her body with each quickening heartbeat.

"What a sweet little man. Beanie you said?" He stroked the infant's fuzzy cheek. Beanie turned and began to root towards Joseph's finger.

Joseph smiled and clucked softly.

"Short for Benjamin," she affirmed. "I guess I'll have to wash my quilt swatch now before I can finish it. Too bad."

They shared a soft giggle.

"He looks to be a pretty big boy. How long is he?"

Rebekah looked at the infant, still safe and snug within Joseph's arm. "I figure about twenty-two or twenty-three inches. Pa will measure him tomorrow against the rope, just as he has done all the others. Then, he will mark it in the kitchen."

Joseph hefted him in his arm. "He certainly isn't a light baby."

A voice from the darkness interrupted their musings. "Here, let me hold my son." Samuel's gentle voice was misty and melodic.

"Oh, ja." Samuel took the child from Joseph. "You weigh more than a ten-pound sack of taters!" His face glowed in the way only a father's could. "I will weigh you in the morning. But you are probably hungry now." He nuzzled the baby, who promptly screeched.

"Thank you, Rebekah," he said as he turned toward his bedroom. "Your Ma is all right, and the baby is all right. All because of you."

She flushed at her father's direct compliment.

"You were an instrument of God's healing tonight, daughter."

Joseph's soft voice deepened her blush. "A true angel."

"Tell Ma I love her," Rebekah whispered. "And I love you, Pa."

Samuel sniffed. "I am a blessed man. Goodnight, Rebekah. Goodnight, Joseph."

When he reached the doorway, he turned again.

"Joseph, do tell the others I won't be back down tonight, but I appreciate their help and I thank God for them. I trust you'll go down to join them soon." Samuel smiled.

Joseph ducked his head. "Yes, sir."

After Samuel retreated to his bedroom, Joseph helped Rebekah back to bed.

"You did a pretty special thing tonight," he whispered as he tucked the cornflower blue quilt in around her.

"Beanie is a pretty special baby." Sleep pulled mercilessly at her eyelids despite his enchanting presence. The cool breeze that fluttered her curtains blew away the tense emotions and excitement. Relaxation consumed her.

"He sure was red," he remembered. "But he wasn't no baby."

She struggled to make sense of his sleep-garbled words. "Huh?"

"At that size, he was a hookin' bull!"

A smile formed on her lips as she gave in to the temptation of sleep. "Beanie Bull," she whispered as her mind danced with the idea of Joseph singing their children to sleep someday.

CHAPTER SEVEN

Beanie Bull's shrill squall met Rebekah's sleepy ears. When she was finally able to force her eyelids open, her room was fuzzy and bright. Pushing herself up in the bed, her heart pounded in time with the baby's urgent cries. As quickly as he began, he quieted.

As the surge of adrenaline ebbed within her, slowing her heartbeat in the sudden quiet, her muscles relaxed.

She rubbed her eyes. "Ma must be feeding him."

A smell that wafted upstairs, though not entirely pleasant, made her lick her lips. Her stomach rumbled.

Rebekah flung the covers back and pushed herself to the side of the bed. She looked at her bruised foot and eased it down onto sunshine-warmed floor.

"It's actually bearable," she said aloud to an absent audience.

She lifted her gown and looked closer. The purple mottling had faded overnight and revealed her own skin color where yesterday, it had been only a mess of green and black. A dark outline was all that remained.

Although her tiny toe wasn't swollen, the nail was solid black. It seemed a little loose, like it might fall off if touched. She wrinkled her nose.

Rebekah grasped the bed frame for support and stood. After a brief rush of tingles from her bad foot, she let go.

"I might not fall." She shifted her weight from foot to foot.

Uncomfortable, but not painful.

She gave her doorframe a wide berth and shuffled to her parent's room.

Elnora's chipper voice surprised her. "Well, there's my best girl."

Beanie lay in the cradle next to the bed, curled like a newborn pup.

"Ma, you look so well." Rebekah couldn't hide her astonishment. Her mother's color had returned and, well, she simply beamed. She eased herself down at the foot of the bed. "You had me quite scared last night."

Despite her forty years, Elnora looked girlish when she smiled. "It's a miracle that you were able to turn your brother."

Her mother shifted her gaze to the sleeping baby. He sighed in his sleep.

Rebekah peered into to the cradle. With one finger, she traced his velvety cheek. He suckled without waking. "Ma, does he look a little yellow?"

"All the boys were yellow, each one a little more than the last. Remember?"

She searched back through her memory. There were very few that didn't contain Joseph in some aspect. Finally, her mind grabbed on to a memory. "Yes, I do remember. We sit them in the window, right?"

Elnora nodded. "In the winter, we put them in the window. Now, we can take him outside. As long as put him into the sunlight often."

"Yes, ma'am. It has been warm for some time now, so I guess we will go outside."

"Your father thinks it will be a mild rest of the season, but I don't think so. I have seen this early warm weather before." Elnora turned her attention to her daughter. After a brief silence, she rose from her bed. "I saw this weather in Germany. I think a change is coming."

Rebekah studied the worried creases across her mother's brow. She had always thought that weather was just that. Weather, plain and simple. They dealt with it accordingly as it came. Cold fingers of fear squeezed her stomach as she watched her mother worry over it so. After all, it was March. Winter was over.

Snapping out of her trance, Elnora gestured to the cradle. "Help your ma push him to the window."

Carefully so as not to wake him, Rebekah helped Elnora situate Beanie in a growing patch of sunlight. With gentle fingers, Elnora peeled back the tiny quilt swatch Joseph brought her the night before. "My quilt is far from done, but it certainly is serving an amazing purpose now, Ma."

Elnora covered her daughter's hand with hers. "It's perfect, my darling. Now…" She stepped back to her bed. Easing down again, she gestured to the door. It appeared to Rebekah that the words simply weren't forming as quickly as Elnora would have liked them to. It was the same after every birth.

"Do bring the shears, please."

Rebekah's hands flew on their own to her singed mane. She groaned. "Oh, Mother, must we cut it all off?"

Elnora's eyes sparkled. "I'll cut it to look just like Joseph's. After all, isn't he taking you to the Spring Festival tonight?"

Rebekah's stomach lurched. "The festival. It's tonight?"

"It is. Now fetch those shears so we can get you ready." Her mother's smile was a tired one. "And we need to introduce Beanie to everyone, don't you think?"

Elnora made short work of Rebekah's haircut. Actually, she made her hair short. After trimming off the mass of melted mane, that which remained danced about her shoulders, light and free. Still, it felt awkward.

Elnora laid the shears on her bedside table. "I believe your green dress will do for tonight, don't you agree, Rebekah?"

She hung her head.

"Come child, what's wrong?" Her mother's hand was light on Rebekah's back.

She sniffled as the unwelcome tears wet her cheeks. "Oh, Mother!"

She turned and buried her face in Elnora's shoulder. "I know I am not supposed to think about how I look, but I can't help it."

Her words came in broken sobs. "My hair is the only thing in the whole village that is different from everybody else. I don't want to look English."

Elnora ran her fingers through the newly-cut hair. "Oh, sweet Rebekah. The Lord doesn't want us to obsess over our appearance, for to Him, we are all his beautiful children. Let me tell you a secret."

Rebekah raised her face and sniffled again. A wisp of blonde fell across her cheek.

"When the Lord made you, he made you beautiful. You're beautiful because you're filled with His love. Nothing on the outside will ever change that." She tucked the stray piece behind Rebekah's ear. "Just between us, I think your hair looks lovely."

Finally, an ounce of gladness crept into her mind. "Thank you, Ma. I just felt so...so..." Her search for the proper word was fruitless, so Rebekah simply shrugged. "I wish I didn't even care about my hair in the first place."

"It was a shock, darling, that's all. You're still my best girl. Now run along so I can get Beanie ready so your father can measure him." She smiled a sweet smile. "See you downstairs, daughter."

Everyone was already downstairs by the time Rebekah, dressed in her favorite green dress, joined them. Her throng of brothers alternated between picking at a loaf of bread and fawning over Beanie, who celebrated the grand meeting by sleeping through it.

Elnora glowed as she and Samuel sat on the loveseat and readied themselves for every question the boys were quivering to fling their way.

"Is this what was going on in the hall last night?"

Elnora started to answer, only to be cut off by another boy.

"How long is he?"

"We're about—" Samuel started, only to be interrupted by yet *another* boy.

"How will you measure him if he can't stand up yet?"

Elnora glanced at her husband and opened her mouth.

"I'll stretch out his legs and you can hold him up."

"No, *I'll* stretch out his legs and *you* can hold him."

"How much does he weigh?"

"How much did *I* weigh?"

Rebekah raised her eyebrows as the questions flew around the sitting room. Her parents didn't seem bothered, though. A knock on their still-closed door drew her attention away from the question-and-question, as opposed to question-and-answer, session.

"I'll get it," she volunteered. Of course, nobody heard her.

Rebekah pulled the door open. Her smile found its usual place as Joseph came into view. "Good morning."

He looked pointedly at his arms, which held an overflowing platter, then back at Rebekah. "I have some food here."

The scent of cinnamon hung thickly on the porch. "I would say you have *all* the food here."

"Ma insisted on having me bake, even in her condition."

"Your Ma is a very sweet woman." Rebekah slid her hand beneath the platter. "Here, let me help you."

Her gaze fluttered back to meet his, where it lingered a moment. Again, her heart began to thunder.

"Mind if I come in and see Beanie?"

How impolite, Rebekah.

"Of course!" She stepped inside with the food. "How is your Ma feeling?"

Joseph held the door and doffed his hat. He nodded as he waded into the fray that was the Stoll household. "She's feeling better. Pa is fixing her a special chair so she can sit at—" He paused before the other words spewed forth in a rush. "At the festival tonight."

Rebekah studied him over her shoulder as she deposited the platter on the table.

Is he blushing?

He stopped beside the loveseat where Elnora still attempted to field questions from the boys. "Did I miss the measuring?"

Elnora shifted so Joseph could see the baby. His face softened at once. "He's bigger than I thought last night."

Samuel appeared from the kitchen, a length of rope in hand. "Every one of you little boys were measured against this rope at birth," he announced as the din quieted. "Then, I hold the rope to the wall and mark the measurement."

The twins looked at each other and nodded. "I never really thought he would get measured standing up," one of them muttered. The voice was so low, it was impossible to tell which had spoken.

Rebekah hid her smile behind her hand at their enlightened expressions.

"Joseph?" Elnora's voice was a little more than a whisper. "Would you like to hold Beanie?"

He nodded emphatically and handed his hat to Rebekah.

Elnora passed Beanie to Joseph and carefully straightened one chubby leg. Samuel pinched the end of the rope at Beanie's head in one finger and measured him, crown to foot. As soon as Elnora released his leg, he curled it back against his body with a tiny sigh.

"Here, I'll take him," Rebekah whispered to Joseph's shoulder.

Ever gentle, he placed the tiny boy into her arms. Their eyes locked. A sizzling heat, like bacon in a skillet, shinnied up Rebekah's backbone.

She tore her gaze away from his and focused on her father as he finished placing Beanie's mark on the wall. Still, her breathing refused to slow.

He spoke first. "Look at that! Already, he is taller than three of his brothers when they were born."

Samuel let out a hoot. "He is a big strapping boy! What did you call him last night, Joseph?"

Joseph shifted a nub of grass from one side of his mouth to the other before he spoke. "Bull. Beanie Bull."

"Ah yes, Beanie Bull," he recited slowly and printed the letters on the doorframe.

Rebekah stepped over to the measuring wall. "Is he bigger than I was, Pa?"

She searched the wall, but her name wasn't near the bottom like everyone else's.

Samuel and Elnora exchanged a look.

"Well, is he?" The smile melted from her face with the silence.

Finally, Samuel spoke. "We didn't start that tradition until Jeremiah was born."

She squatted carefully and studied the wall. Sure enough, there was her first mark.

REBEKAH – AGED 7

"Oh, I see." Her knotted brow eased. "Well, if we're counting first marks, then I was taller than all of you."

The choir of boys disagreed in a mishmash of tenors and basses.

Rebekah stepped to her father's side. "Well, how big is this little hookin' bull?"

Samuel waved his hands. A slow hush fell over his boys. Once they were quiet, Rebekah slipped Beanie into his arm. "The new baby is twenty-three inches long. And weighs…"

Joseph handed him a sack filled with potatoes. Samuel hefted Beanie in one arm and the sack in the other. "A little more than a ten-pound sack of potatoes! I'd say twelve pounds."

Samuel stood, beaming, with his sack of spuds and his newborn babe. The little boys milled about before drifting en masse outdoors.

Elnora smiled and took a seat in the sitting room. "My, that was an event." She motioned to Rebekah and Joseph. "Come, sit. Are you two excited for the festival tonight?"

"Yes, ma'am." Joseph avoided Rebekah's glance as he took the seat across from her mother. "My ma's been baking since last night to prepare for it."

Elnora eased back on the loveseat. "We've been soaking apples—"

Her tired eyes widened. "At least I hope somebody put the apples in to soak, because I honestly don't remember doing it."

Rebekah giggled. "Pa put them in to soak yesterday…I think."

After sharing a laugh, a quick screech from Beanie brought Elnora to her feet. "Well, children, I believe Beanie and I better go nap before the festivities tonight."

Joseph rose when she did.

The woman's voice was tinted with exhaustion. "Won't you bake the pies, Rebekah?"

"I will, Ma."

After watching Elnora and Beanie retreat up the stairs, Joseph turned back to Rebekah. He plucked his hat from somewhere and danced from foot to foot.

She reached to scratch a rogue itch behind her ear.

I've never seen him so jittery.

A piece of newly cut hair brushed across her cheek. She froze.

My hair. He must be put off by my hair.

A sensation of creepy-crawlies, just beneath the skin, scurried down her arms.

Joseph cleared his throat. "Well, I'd better get home." Still turning his hat in his hands, he shuffled to the door. He spoke again without turning to face her. "I'll come for you before dinner, if that's all right with you."

"That'll be fine. I'll see you then."

Without a goodbye, he hesitated only a moment before he pulled the door shut behind him.

CHAPTER EIGHT

Puzzled, Rebekah stared at the closed door.

He's never acted so strange before.

Cold knots of uncertainty formed in her stomach. She started toward the kitchen with her hands wrung at her waist.

"Pa? Are you in here, Pa?"

Samuel's voice came from outside. "Go on. Get out of here!"

Rebekah lifted her skirt and hurried to see what brought on the commotion.

Sure enough, there was Pa outside the back door. He had put the apples to soak in the wooden barrel as she recalled. However, in all the excitement, he had neglected to put the lid on. There were the twins, bobbing away amid the apples.

"Look Pa, we got to swim and snack." Each boy grasped a thoroughly-gnawed core in their chubby hands.

The boys, though, weren't where Samuel's squawking was aimed. His new draft horses, bought just the day before from Mr. Yoder, had helped themselves to the apples as well.

"Ma's not going to be happy about this," Rebekah muttered as she stepped out to join her family.

Samuel stood with his hands on his head as his horses trotted back toward his new barn. She could hear them crunching their stolen apples.

She drew a hand to her mouth in a poor attempt to stifle a

giggle as Jeremiah plucked the boys from the apple barrel. Her attempt to hold back the laughter didn't work.

"Oh, Pa!" she managed between giggles. "I'll start the pies with the apples we have left."

Her father's brown hair stuck out from his head in angry wisps. "That Mr. Yoder. He didn't tell me dem horses had a taste for da apples."

His German accent thickened with his mood.

The twins dashed by in a sea of giggles, just shy of Jeremiah's reach.

"Thank you for putting them in to soak, Pa. What with all the commotion lately. . ."

Joseph.

Rebekah twisted her fingers together. "It's a wonder any of us can think at all."

Samuel looped his arm around her shoulder. "Jeremiah can get the boys cleaned up and ready. Who knew the apple barrel was the best place to take a swim?" He gave her a quick squeeze. "It does my heart glad to know you're going to the festival tonight on the arm of Joseph Graber. He's a fine young man, he is."

She studied the ground. The strings of her covering dangled in her vision and drew her attention to any menial thing that *wasn't* talking about Joseph Graber with her Pa. "It's good you're pleased."

Samuel patted her shoulder. "Go get to baking, daughter. We can get a handful of pies made if we start now."

"We?"

Samuel ran his thumbs along the inside of his black braces. "I was a mighty fine pie maker back in Germany. I baked a pie for your ma when we were courting."

Rebekah cocked an eyebrow. "Ma never mentioned that."

"Oh ja, I'll never forget the look on her face when she tried that first bite. Her eyes might near popped right out of her head."

Forgetting her anxiety over Joseph, she stared at her father in disbelief. "It was that good?"

Samuel rubbed his chin. "Her exact words were, 'You mixed up the salt and the sugar. Good thing I know the difference, otherwise we could never host any families in our home.'" Samuel's glance cut to his daughter. "I asked her to marry me that night, and thankfully, she said yes."

"Oh, Pa, that is the sweetest story."

He shrugged. "I don't know about sweetest. I figured it to be the saltiest."

The sun crept from the east to the west with all the sluggishness of a snail. By the time the pies cooled on the front porch, all the boys were dressed in their Sunday best and ready to go.

Elnora fussed over Beanie's outfit while Rebekah and Samuel tidied the kitchen.

"Thanks for letting me help, daughter."

She stowed the white sugar back in the safety of the highest cabinet, far away from grabby boy fingers. "Thank you for letting me measure out the salt and sugar."

They shared an easy laugh as the evening birds began their nightly song.

Samuel twirled a rag around his hand. "Young Joseph should be here soon."

Rebekah froze.

Her father's words were as soft as the spring rain. "No matter what happens tonight, Rebekah, follow your heart. Your mother and I want nothing more than your happiness."

He gave the rag a fling. It landed expertly in the dry sink.

Before she could contemplate her father's heartfelt words, Jeremiah stuck his head in the kitchen. "Joseph's here."

With his lips pulled into his most mischievous grin, he stared directly at his sister. "Joseph's here. And boy, does he look pretty."

Rebekah tugged at her cape. Satisfied that it was situated, she straightened her covering. Then, she smoothed her dress.

"Are you going to leave him waiting for you all night?" Jeremiah pressed.

Finally, she sucked in a deep breath and swept past her biggest little brother. "Of course not, silly."

Everyone had congregated in the sitting room, but she spotted Joseph in a moment. A head taller than even her father, he stood out in a crowd. She chewed her lower lip as she beheld the sight of him laughing and teasing with her mother.

His black felt special-occasion hat was clutched in one hand while the other was tucked securely in a pocket. Those ebony curls that never failed to grab her attention were slicked back and he wore his deep-green shirt, the one that matched her favorite dress. He was long, lean, and in Rebekah's eyes, most beautiful.

"My mother and father took our food on to the festival," he explained. "Do Rebekah and I need to take any of the pies for you?"

Samuel offered his hand to the younger man. "I appreciate the offer, but I believe we can handle those pies."

Carefully, Joseph removed his hand from his pocket and shook Samuel's hand. Quickly, he tucked it away again.

"Hallo." Rebekah was aware that her voice was quiet, but Joseph took instant notice. He stepped through the throng of little brothers and joined her.

He's so tall he could have stepped over the lot of them.

His eyes were especially blue as he offered her his arm. "Shall we go?"

Her cheeks afire, Rebekah flitted a glance to Elnora, only her mother wasn't looking at them. Instead, she shared a smile with Samuel. Together, they turned their attention to the young couple.

What is going on? Why so much secrecy tonight?

Following Joseph, mostly because she held his arm, they made their way out the front door.

Just before the door closed, Elnora's voice met Rebekah's ears. "We will see you there."

Then, she and Joseph were alone.

The festival was a wonderful gathering of friends and family and, once he had gotten over his initial shyness or whatever had him so out of sorts, Joseph was a perfect gentleman. For Rebekah, being with him was as easy and natural as getting honey from a beehive. The few looks Katie tossed their way were easy enough to ignore. Still, it was no secret that the younger of the Knepp twins spent the evening wishing *she* had arrived on Joseph's arm.

Rebekah twirled the clover thistle that Joseph picked for her on the way between her fingers. "Thank you for a lovely night."

The evening of food, fun, and fellowship—and, of course, being near to Joseph—left her starry-eyed and a little giddy.

"I should be the one thanking you. If it hadn't been for you, I wouldn't have had a soul to drink apple cider with." He rubbed his belly with one hand. "And to share that last piece of your ma's apple pie. If I had been forced to finish it all alone, my folks may well have had to roll me home."

She dipped her head to sniff her thistle and to hide her smile. "Actually, Pa and I made the pies this year. Ma wasn't feeling up to it yet."

"I thought they tasted a little extra-cinnamony." Joseph bent and scooped up a rock. "I must say, Rebekah, you certainly got all of her skill in the kitchen." He flung the rock into the woods and it thunked against a tree. "All of it and then some."

"You're awfully complimentary tonight, Joseph Graber."

He grinned. "Could you get used to it?"

"Maybe."

Something bumped her hand. "Oh!"

"What is it?"

"Something bumped me." She shuddered.

"Something like this?" Under the cover of darkness, Joseph's hand bumped hers again. This time, though, his fingers twined around hers and linked them together.

A wave of shyness swept over her. Her hand trembled and her stomach knotted. How she'd dreamt of the day when he would take her hand in his or even brush against her. In her daydreams, it was always wonderful. But this moment left her daydreams all behind.

"Looks like your folks set the lanterns out for you," Joseph observed. "It was a shame they had to leave the festival early."

Though she wanted to respond and continue the jovial conversation with Joseph, who was obviously now her beau, she didn't trust her own tongue just yet.

Indifferent to her lack of words, he continued. "I suppose Elnora didn't want little Beanie Bull to catch a chill." Finishing his theory as they reached the porch, he pulled her close, their hands still intertwined. His other hand was hidden in his far pocket. The lamplight glinted off his eyes and them appear to be nothing more than a sea of azure sparkles.

"Rebekah, there's something I'd like to talk to you about." The resolve in Joseph's strong voice wavered. "It's no secret—"

Something cracked from the understory. Joseph froze and both he and Rebekah swiveled their heads in the direction of the noise.

"Well, well, well. What have we here?" Slowly, Peter emerged from the woods.

Joseph squared his shoulders at the perceived threat. "Now's not the appropriate time to come for your wagon."

A sliver of ice slid down Rebekah's backbone at Joseph's tone. Had she been a man, she would have backed off. As things were, though, she felt that she was in awfully capable hands.

Peter leaned and spat as he stepped nearer to them. "I'm not here for the wagon right now. I'm not here for you neither." His spurs jangled, and a swift breeze blew back his duster to reveal the shiny pistols that hung there.

Joseph slipped his hand from Rebekah's, which had grown suddenly sweaty. She linked hers behind her back and shrank behind him.

"Then I don't see as you have any business here at this hour at all." Had Joseph been a cat, his tail would have been bottle-brushy.

Peter ignored him and shifted his steely stare to Rebekah. "I need to speak to you."

Rebekah shook her head infinitesimally.

"It's important."

The door to the house squeaked open. "Hallo, Peter. Did I hear you mention you needed to speak to my daughter?"

Samuel rested his hands with his thumbs on the inside of his black braces.

"Yessir."

Samuel nodded. "I see. However, it is much too late and, Rebekah, you should be getting on to bed. Joseph, you come in, too. Your Pa is here." Samuel motioned toward the door. "Peter, won't you come back in the morning? Breakfast is at six. You can talk to Rebekah about what's on your mind then."

Peter nodded. "Settled, then." He spat a brown stream into the yard. "You bet I'll be back."

"Joseph, your pa is in the sitting room. He figured you'd walk Rebekah home and may like a ride to your place." Samuel's voice revealed no trace of any nervousness he might felt at Peter's display. Rebekah's wasn't as calm.

"Goodnight, Joseph. Thank you again for a wonderful evening." She tried not to bite off her farewell, but not only was her pa right there, but the romantic moment, illuminated by moonlight and lanterns, was forgotten. She started up the stairs, careful of the creaky one.

"I'll see you for breakfast, Rebekah."

She paused in her ascent. "You'll be here, too?"

Joseph stared up at her. She hadn't intended for her question to sound gruff but judging by the way the smile melted from his dimpled face, it had.

She forced a grateful smile and stammered to undo her mistake. "Then I'll be sure to have cinnamon rolls ready."

Following her lead, Joseph returned her smile. "See you then."

Rebekah turned and finished climbing the stairs. Adrenaline surged through her veins as she replayed the conversation with Peter in her mind.

What could he have to say to me?

Rebekah walked past her bedroom and instead, found herself in her quilting room. Easing into her rocker, she plucked up her quilting bag.

"Sweet Ma. She must have placed my sad excuse for a quilt in my bag in the off chance I wanted to practice my sorely lacking skills."

She knows me so well.

With her emotions a swirling tempest, she began to stitch by moonlight.

CHAPTER NINE

Peter's voice was harsh in the early morning light. "You invited me back and here I am, though I wish you had allowed me to speak last night."

His mouth was a hard line as he stared at Rebekah from beneath his hat. The scar above his eye gave him a fierce look, but she wasn't afraid, despite the presence of the pistols on his hips.

Curious, she'd decided last night beneath the moonlight. But not afraid.

Joseph appeared at her side. "Breakfast is on the table. Won't you come in and join us?"

Peter huffed. "I ought to have known you'd be here." Slowly, he removed his hat. "Yes, I believe I will." Stepping between them, he walked with confidence to the table.

Elnora and Samuel rose politely.

"You can sit here," Rebekah whispered. She touched the back of a chair. Peter nodded.

Easing around the table, she took the seat next to Joseph and across from Peter. An uneasy silence blanketed the table that, moments before, had been bustling.

Samuel spoke first. "We've already blessed this meal, Peter, so you are welcome to help yourself."

Peter ran a hand through his blond mane. "Much obliged." He picked up the plate Rebekah had set for him and pointed to a tin which sat just out of reach. "Biscuit, please."

Careful to keep her face expressionless, she passed the biscuits. Joseph even ignored the special cinnamon rolls she'd made especially for him. Still, no one spoke.

After dumping two ladles of gravy over the fluffy pastries, Peter finally sighed. "I reckon I'll simply say what I've come to say."

He focused his burning stare on Rebekah. "I came before 'cause I heard tell it might be true and I had to see for myself. Now, I know that it is."

Rebekah cut her eyes to Joseph, who sat nearer to her than usual. The warmth radiating from his body was comforting, as though he would protect her no matter what important piece of news Peter had brought.

He glanced back at her and their eyes locked for a brief moment.

Thank goodness we are in this together.

"Two decades ago, a family came across the Pike in a covered wagon. They left their home in Philadelphia, packed what they could, and headed west."

Elnora dropped her fork. It met her breakfast plate in a clatter. Rebekah looked at her, but her mother didn't retrieve the fork. Samuel reached across and laid a hand on his wife's arm.

Ma is trembling.

Peter waited until everyone was quiet before he continued.

"A woman named Sara and her husband Wesley were driving the wagon. In the back was the older brother, and Hannah, the baby. Not too far from this place right here, there was an accident."

Rebekah leaned forward, her eyebrows knitted together.

"Sara and Wesley were killed. It seems they collided with a runaway wagon. Those folks were killed, too."

Rebekah was powerless to stem her curiosity. "What about the children?"

Peter laced his fingers over his plate. He continued his recitation as though he'd practiced it for years.

Or decades.

"The boy lived. He was about seven years of age and by some miracle, a passing wagon picked him up as he was running back east. That wagon was headed to Pennsylvania, so they took the boy in."

"And the girl?" Rebekah's voice was a whisper.

"It was thought that she was killed, too. But one day, when the boy was all grown up, he came looking for his sister. See…" Peter ran his hand through his hair again. "Those folks who took the boy east were old. They died when he was still only a spud, so that sister is the only family he's got in the world."

Elnora still hadn't looked up. Even the throng of boys was quiet.

"I figured the first place to start looking was the scene of the accident. A youngster by the name of Elijah, I believe, sure had a belly-load of answers for all my questions. He's the one pointed me this way."

Joseph's fist clenched and unclenched in his lap.

Rebekah leaned back in her chair. "So, what are you saying, Peter?"

The man glanced at the faces around the breakfast table. "Well, what I'm saying is—"

Elnora's voice was so quiet it would have gone unheard if not for the deafening stillness of the room. "It was an Indian attack that killed those folks. Not a runaway wagon."

Peter sucked in a deep breath and nodded.

Samuel pushed his chair back from the table, making everyone jump in unison.

Peter paid him no mind and shifted his gaze to Rebekah. "I'm that boy."

Rebekah kept her face expressionless as her father rose from his seat. Following suit, Joseph rose, too.

Samuel's normally melodic voice was flat. "I think you'd better leave now."

The visitor pushed back from the table and looked first at Joseph, then at Samuel. "You boys gonna throw me out then?" He smiled. "It'd take a whole lot more of you than this."

Slowly, he stood.

Joseph's face was contorted in planes Rebekah had never seen before. "No, we're not throwing you out. You're leaving on your own. Now come on."

The two men moved around opposite sides of the table and

herded Peter to the front door.

Jamming his hat on his head, he waved his hands in mock defeat. "You boys win."

Rebekah stood. Peter locked eyes with her over Joseph's shoulder. "You're not Rebekah. Your name is Hannah and you're my sister."

Joseph slammed the door, but it was too late.

The men hovered near the door as Rebekah searched for someone to help her make sense of the Peter's strange tale.

"Is it true, Ma?"

Elnora, who hadn't looked up from her lap since she'd dropped her fork, sniffled. The sobs, which had been quiet, now came long and loud. They tore from her mother like screams from a laboring woman.

Slowly, Rebekah turned. "Pa?"

She searched his face as the tears welled in her eyes. Hating her weakness, she swiped at them with the back of her hand. "Is it true, Pa? Am I not even your daughter?"

"Rebekah, we never meant to—"

The tears she'd willed not to fall spilled over and hung in her lashes until they dropped onto her cheeks. Anger flashed within her as she turned her face toward the ceiling. "Never meant to what? Lie to me? Never meant to correct me when I called you Father and Mother?"

Thomas released a sob. "Stop it, sissy, you're scaring me."

She ignored him and flickered her hot stare to Joseph. "You knew about this all along, didn't you?"

He recoiled as though she'd slapped him.

"That's enough." Elnora dabbed her face with a hanky and silenced her sobs. "The Grabers knew about this. Everyone did." Her voice was serious. "But Joseph was only a baby when your pa and I found you, naked and hungry, under a bush."

Rebekah drew in a shuddering breath. "Everyone knows about this? Everyone but *me*?" The anger threatened to flare again.

"Rebekah, you'll take your seat, or you'll leave this table. Understood?"

She dropped her gaze coolly to meet Elnora's. "This isn't *my* table."

Rebekah left her breakfast dishes untouched and stalked

across the sitting area. When she reached the door, she stopped.
Samuel stepped aside. Glimmering tears flecked his eyelashes.
Joseph had already gone.

She kept her voice low so that only Samuel could hear. "I'll
be— I'll be—" She blew out a haughty breath and grasped the
doorknob. "Oh, I don't know where I'll be." She marched out the
door and let it slam behind her.

"There is not one person I can turn to right now." Tears ran in
rivulets down her cheeks. The weight of Peter's words grew
heavier by the moment, and if Rebekah didn't confide in someone
soon, she feared she might explode.

She lifted her skirt and ran until she heard it. The soft sounds
of someone who would understand. Someone who didn't already
know the whole sordid story. Someone who hadn't kept it from
her.

She flung herself into the sweet-smelling hay and wrapped her
arms around Buttermilk's neck. Burying her face in the calf's
warm hide, she sobbed until there were no more tears left to cry.
With those out of the way, she could finally talk.

"Oh, Buttermilk, why did this have to happen? And now of all
times?"

The tiny calf craned her neck to look at her. "Blehhhh."

"They lied to me all these years, Buttermilk. They *lied*."

A twig popped. Her already pounding heart skipped a beat.
"They didn't lie, Rebekah. They merely never told you."

Joseph ambled over, a sprig of grass in his teeth.

She swiped at her face. It felt puffy and a bit soggy. "Did you
know, Joseph? And please don't lie."

He squatted and looked her squarely in the eye. "No. I didn't
know."

Rebekah flicked a potato bug off her dress. The calf leaned to
investigate it. "If you had known, would you have told me?"

"Of course."

She shoved her hand under a scattering of hay. "Really?"

"Really. I have never kept anything from you, Rebekah, and I
never will."

She sighed. "What am I supposed to do now?"

Joseph folded his lanky frame into the straw beside her. "Are you asking me or Buttermilk?"

Her heart was too heavy to smile at his gentle joke. "You."

He picked up a long stick of straw and commenced doodling in the dirt. "Well, since you asked, I'll tell you. First thing you need to do is talk to God. Then, you need to apologize to your parents for the way you treated them. After that, talk to your brothers, especially Thomas. They love you so and are innocent in all of this."

Content with his speech, Joseph dropped the straw.

Rebekah couldn't fathom an answer. The emptiness was too much. She simply watched the dust motes drift their twirly dance in the bright sunrays in the barn's door. "Can we go for a walk?"

Joseph stood and offered her his hand. "Of course. You should tell your parents we are going, though. No doubt they're worried."

Lacing her fingers together, she stared at them. "Perhaps you could tell them for me?"

He nodded and turned toward the house. Her house. Where she'd lived, made memories, made mistakes, and been loved. Her house, where she'd delivered the newest Stoll baby. Where she'd prayed, quilted, and worshipped. Fresh feelings of stabbing pain filled her chest. With her eyes closed, Rebekah started toward the lake.

A moment later, Joseph caught up. It didn't take long with his lengthy strides in comparison to her shorter, unfocused ones. "Your parents send a message. They asked me to tell you that when you're ready to talk, they'll be there."

She turned her face up to him. "Thank you. I will, when I have the right words."

He nodded. There was no evidence of any sort of smile on his handsome face. "They also said to tell you that they love you. And that the decision to go back and live English or stay here with us is yours and yours alone. They'll respect it, either way."

He shoved his hands in his pockets.

Even if his hand had brushed hers, as it had last night, she wouldn't have felt up to holding it anyway. She eased herself down on the bank and hugged her knees to her chest.

Before long, the honey-like scent of the tulip tree, the one he'd used to carve their fishing poles, filled the air.

That seems like a lifetime ago now.

A couple of birds chittered back and forth in perfect singsong time, but Rebekah didn't try to pick out what kind they were. Her heart was simply too heavy.

"Rebekah, there is something—" Joseph fidgeted in his pockets and shifted his weight from foot to foot. "We were about to speak of it last night when Peter came, but I really feel I need to say it now, if you'll let me."

She stared out over the glistening water. A fish jumped and sent a splashing ripple across the lake. "Okay, Joseph."

None of the enthusiasm from the previous night could be found in her words.

His gaze burned on the exposed skin of her neck as he sat carefully beside her. Still, she didn't meet his eyes. "I have feelings for you, Rebekah. You and only you."

Rebekah's heart thudded in her chest. She wanted to be excited to hear these words from the lips of the man who'd stolen her heart so long ago, but there was too much new information to process to even allow the moment to be enjoyable. Tears pricked her eyes as Joseph proceeded to unburden his heart of all the right words at the completely wrong time.

"The more I've prayed about them—and about you—the stronger these feelings have grown." Still, his stare burned on her skin.

He is willing me to look up.

She didn't.

She couldn't.

"They've been building for years, Rebekah." Slowly, he placed his hand on hers.

Please, don't continue.

Rebekah kept her hand immovable beneath his. "Joseph—" She pressed her hand deeper into the soft dirt.

This particular spot would be perfect for worm hunting if we were here to fish.

Not one to be deterred, Joseph stroked her fingers with his. "What I'm trying to say is that I love you, Rebekah."

His words echoed over the water and hung there between

them in the still spring air.

A lone tear slid down her cheek. "Joseph, Samuel and Elnora have always told all us kids what love was. They said people make it more difficult but that a real, lasting love is really simple." She pulled both her hands into her lap and left Joseph's alone in the dirt. She didn't bother to wipe away the tear before she finally turned to face him. "Love is understanding."

Joseph bobbed his head. "My parents have said the same thing."

Rebekah could see the uncertainty in his eyes and having to say words that would cause him pain burned at the raw ends of her already broken heart. "I can't love you if I don't love myself…not the kind of love you deserve."

Rebekah stood and stepped toward the lake, unable to watch while she didn't return his profession of the world's most precious sentiment. "And I don't understand anything right now, especially not myself."

He was silent.

"I'm sorry, Joseph. I can't love and understand you if I don't love and understand myself."

With a tear-streaked face, she finally turned away from the water. Joseph, though, was no longer there.

Rebekah sank to the ground and folded her arms across her knees. Broken sobs tore from her throat, resonating from the depths of her very soul. Her shoulders shook, and the tears were never ending.

I forced Joseph away, my oldest friend in the world. Now, I'm truly all alone.

The sun had already begun its daily rush toward the western horizon by the time Rebekah felt able to head back to the Stoll homestead. With steps as painfully slow as she could muster, Rebekah trudged across a field of wheat that bordered the English road that led to Montgomery. Never before had she ever dared walk this close to the road and never alone.

Before she got halfway across the waving wheat field, an English wagon came into view. The sounds of laughing children in the wagon bed tinkled through the air, much like the happy sound of water trickling in a creek.

Rebekah's pulse thudded in her ears.

Should I run or should I hide here in the wheat?

Before she could decide, a movement from the opposite end of the road caught her eye. Her heart skipped a beat when she realized it was an Amish buggy.

She studied the buggy for a moment.

That's Katie and Annie's buggy. A wide grin parted her lips and for a moment, she thought about waving. The girls were nowhere in sight. Only their father sat in the driver's box.

Mr. Knepp must be heading back to Gasthof Village from selling his hand-hewn chairs in Montgomery.

A thought burst into Rebekah's mind so quickly, she sprinted forward a few steps.

Maybe he can give me a ride home.

Before she could wave or call out, the horse pulling the Knepp buggy stumbled and fell.

Adrenaline surged as a sickening knot formed in her throat, then sank to the pit of her stomach. The smile that had been on her lips melted into a frown.

Slowing politely, the English wagon crept past the Amish buggy.

Oh, not Mr. Knepp. God, why? Why would tragedy befall him, a man of the gentlest sort?

Heat burned in Rebekah's cheeks and neck. "I cannot be one of them! They didn't even stop to help." Her angry rant through clenched teeth trailed off into the Indiana breeze as the English wagon ground to a halt in the road.

Curiosity cooled her burst of fear and Rebekah watched as the driver got down and trotted back to inspect Mr. Knepp's horse.

"She's lame," the Englishman called out. His words were laced with a strange accent. The musical laughter of the English children ceased as the man's wife climbed down and unhooked one of their horses from the wagon.

Rebekah's jaw dropped as the Englishman, whistling a jolly tune that carried on the breeze, proceeded to help Mr. Knepp's old mare up and tied her to the back of the Amish buggy before he hooked his own horse up carefully to the front.

When he'd finished, he stuck out his hand to Mr. Knepp. The pair nodded at each other before the Englishman rejoined his family in his wagon and continued on his way.

Or perhaps I could.

A lone tear trickled down her cheek.

She glanced at the horizon where the sun sank lower still.

Tonight, by moonlight, I will take the long way home.

An owl, no doubt hunting for a meal, hooted as she passed beneath a low-hanging branch. Rebekah clutched her cape tighter about her shoulders. Normally, such an unexpected sound under the cover of darkness would have frightened her, but not tonight. Tonight, she was on her own.

A skunk, mostly white and unlike those she'd seen, skittered along the bank of the stream. "Good evening, little skunk."

She watched as the smallish creature ran, her coat gleaming in the moon's rays. "You look so soft."

The skunk paused to sniff at a clump of reeds.

"You've always known who you are, what you are, and where you come from." She watched as the animal disappeared into the understory. "Not like me."

A voice came to her, as soft and gentle as the night's breeze. *You love me and I love you. I will always be with you, and always love you, no matter what name you choose to go by.*

Rebekah felt the words in her heart as much as she heard them in her mind.

A beaver eased into the water from his slide on the riverbank. A pair of night birds chittered overhead. There, amid some of God's most innocent creatures, Rebekah began to pray aloud.

"Thank you, Father. I know you will always remain faithful, as will I. But what should I do? I am not who I thought I was. I chose not to live with the English on Rumspringa and yet I *am* English."

You are Rebekah Stoll, loved by Elnora and Samuel. And Joseph.

"But Father, they lied—"

And Peter. You are loved by Peter, too.

Rebekah considered this and quickened her steps. "Is it all right to love Joseph back?"

Nothing has changed. You are still you, Joseph is still him. He gave his heart to you with my blessing and after much prayer.

"Oh, Father, but I've pushed all my family away, the only family I've ever known." Rebekah lifted her skirt and began to jog. "I wish I had taken the short way home." She swept along the path, breathing in the air that had taken on a chill. Her covering strings flounced about. "Please forgive me, Father. I am sorry for having acted selfishly."

She slowed her running and dropped to her knees. Clasping her hands together at her chin, Rebekah closed her eyes. "I ask for forgiveness in Jesus' name. Please give me the words to apologize to my parents. I love them so and never meant to hurt them. And to Joseph. Amen."

The peaceful voice was there again. *Never forget who you are, Rebekah Stoll. Go forth and show my love in your actions, in your words, and in your thoughts.*

Tears of humble gratitude shimmered on her lashes. "Thank you, Father."

Rebekah rose and hurried along the path, but a foreign sound distracted her. In the understory, something was struggled, shaking the leaves on a low shrub. Whatever it was whimpered.

Rebekah knelt and pulled back a limber branch with one hand. There, with a snare around its paw, stood a large porcupine. She released the branch and scurried backward.

"Pa says not to go near porcupine," she told the stuck creature from the safety of the other side of the leaves. "Those quills will hurt."

It whimpered again, soft and helpless.

Two little shadows emerged from under the bush.

"Oh!" Rebekah let her eyes adjust to the falling darkness. "Are these your babies?"

Two tiny quilled creatures milled about and didn't stray far from their mother. The porcupine whimpered again.

"The English must have set snares, though I can't figure why. Pa mentioned people called trappers once, but I've never seen one." Gingerly, she pulled the branch back again. The animal tugged at the snare. She succeeded only in making it tighter.

Show my love in your actions to all my creatures.

Rebekah crouched and held the branch back with her body, while taking care not to squash any baby porcupines. "All right, mama, I'm talk to you while I set you free from that snare."

The large porcupine stood motionless, her dark eyes studying Rebekah's every move.

God, help me.

She eased her hands forward. "Now, mama, I'll lift you up so I can loosen that snare. Don't be scared, though. I'm scared enough for both of us."

Cautiously, she slid her hands beneath the prickly animal.

"Good job, mama." Shifting her weight, she held the hefty animal against her side with one hand and worked the snare free from her paw with the other. "Now, we're almost done, and you'll be free to go on your way with your family."

Family.

Rebekah ignored the sheen of sweat that had formed on her neck and eased the heavy animal back to the ground. "All done."

The mother porcupine's large nostrils flared as she breathed in the human's scent. Her babies still meandered around, oblivious to the goings on. Pressing her flat face against Rebekah's hand, the animal made a *whuff* before she turned away.

She sucked in her lower lip, waiting for any quills to fly. They didn't. The large porcupine, who weighed about as much as Beanie, lumbered into the woods with her babies trailing behind her.

Through me, all things are possible.

"Even coming back from this mess is possible," Rebekah reasoned aloud. "If I can free a wild animal from a trap, I can get over being human."

Enthusiasm filled her mind, replacing the emptiness, fear, and resentment that had threatened to consume her. Suddenly eager to get home, Rebekah jerked the snare from the ground and stuffed it into her dress pocket. Two more sat nearby, undisturbed. She snatched those free, too.

"Thank you, Father," she prayed aloud. Her steps quickened to a run. "Thank you!"

CHAPTER TEN

The house was dark when Rebekah sprinted into the familiar clearing. The moon, high and bright, gave plenty of light to find her way home. Rebekah crept through the back door.

Please don't let me wake anybody up.

The doorframe boasting all the measurements of the Stoll children seemed to stare at her; an impassible obstacle that had to be defeated before she could make her final decision.

Taking a deep breath, Rebekah straightened her covering and marched to the marked wall. "I'm blessed to have been included in this family," she told the wall. "And I'll be thankful forever that I have been."

That task completed, she crept up the stairs and took care to step over the squeaky one that Samuel kept intending to fix. Instead of slipping into the safety of her hand-hewn quilts that were stacked neatly atop her bed, she slipped into her quilting room.

There, her quilting bag lay haphazardly where she'd left it after when she'd become irritated with her irregular stitching. Her quilt section lay across it, untouched, beside her rocking chair. Rebekah strode across the room and flung the curtains back. The silvery moonbeams cascaded in, giving her ample light by which to quilt. "I will finish this project tonight. It has dragged on long enough."

She plopped into her rocking chair and snatched up the quilt piece with newfound fervor. *This one was a gift from Katie Knepp* she thought as she reached into her bag and pulled out a square.

"I must love Katie as I love myself, even if she is sweet on Joseph. All those feelings are gone; this new and improved Rebekah Stoll is here to stay."

When the silvery moonlight gave way to the soft-hued rays of the sun, Rebekah was putting the finishing touches on her long-awaited quilt. She hadn't slept, but she'd never felt more awake in all her twenty years.

She rose wide-eyed from the rocker with the finished quilt displayed before her at arm's length.

Perfectly imperfect.

She packed the few remaining squares neatly into her bag and stowed it in her room before folding her first handmade quilt into a neat pile.

The sounds and smells of breakfast being prepared met her on the stairs. With her project draped over her arm, she took the first steps into her life as the new and improved, but still a work-in-progress, Rebekah Stoll.

She hovered in the kitchen doorway, savoring the sight before her. None of her brothers were downstairs yet, or if some were, they were already out in the barn, busy with their chores.

Samuel had moved Beanie's cradle downstairs and the baby, still tinted slightly yellow, soaked up the rays of sunshine provided by the window. Elnora sliced the cinnamon-filled dough for breakfast rolls while Samuel hefted wood into the cookstove.

Please, Lord, give me the words.

"Good morning Ma. Pa." Rebekah's greeting seemed to fill the expanse that was their kitchen. Elnora froze, as did Samuel.

Her mother placed the slicing knife on the counter and turned slowly. Her eyes, normally sparkly, were red-rimmed and watery and her nose was rosy. Samuel turned too. His haggard face wore the same red-rimmed expression as his wife's.

"I have something to say to both of you." Surprisingly, her voice didn't sound meek but confident. "I was wrong to speak to you in such a manner. To accuse you and resent you. I was wrong.

I asked God for forgiveness, now I'm asking for yours."

Elnora's lower lip began to tremble as she held her arms out wide. "Come here, daughter."

Rushing into her mother's waiting arms, Rebekah felt the same peace as she had the night before. A moment later, Samuel's strong embrace circled them both.

"I love you both, I am sorry I was angry at you…all you did was love me." Despite the peace, a fresh cascade of healing tears spilled from her eyes. Her mother's frame shook with quiet sobs.

Samuel was the first to release from the group hug. "We prayed, too. Your mother and I should have told you the truth sooner and almost did on many occasions."

He glanced at Elnora, who stepped back from the hug and dabbed at her soggy cheeks with a hanky. "But we simply never did."

"We tried to do right by you, daughter, and to raise you no different to our boys." Her mother reached one thin hand to Rebekah. She took it. "But you are different."

She nodded. "Now that I know I am English, I will learn to embrace it."

Elnora smiled the knowing smile only a mother can produce. "Darling girl. That is not what I meant. You're different because you're our eldest child and our only girl. You, my dear, are our little miracle."

Rebekah had expected to be reminded that she was indeed of English blood, but Elnora's words left her shocked. Humble, simple love of the purest form filled her heart for her mother, her father, and her people.

"I love you Ma, Pa." Rebekah lifted the finished quilt and held it out before her. "I finished it last night, Ma."

The squares were uneven and jagged, held together by awkward stitches. The border was larger in some places than others, and the whole conglomeration wasn't so much square as it was sort of oval. The filling was oddly-placed and the backing…well, the backing was comprised of three different colors of fabric instead of one uniform one, like Elnora's.

She studied her parent's reactions as they, in turn, studied her quilt-like product.

"This quilt is me," Rebekah whispered. "Not perfect, not by a long shot. But it is filled with memories, love, and lots and lots of try."

A tear dripped from the corner of Elnora's eye. "Daughter, it is beautiful. I am so proud of you for finishing it."

"I'd like to give it to my newest little brother, since it was the first article to touch him as he arrived here in our home."

"Thank you, daughter." Moving lightly, she draped the quilt over the end of his cradle. "I'll wrap him in it when he's finished his sun bath."

Her parents exchanged a look. "We love you, Rebekah. We always will, no matter if you choose to stay with us or go back with Peter to the English."

Her eyes widened. Had she neglected to mention the best part of her decision? "Oh, Ma, I'm not going anywhere. This is my home. I'll never leave!"

A sigh escaped her mother's lips as her free hand fluttered to her belly. "Thank you, Lord," she whispered. "Thank you for this being Your will."

With a contagious grin, Rebekah skipped toward the back door. "I can't wait to tell my brothers."

Samuel stepped toward her. "Rebekah, the boys have gone down to the lake to fish. Thomas wanted fish for lunch."

"I'll go down and find them." She placed her hand on the doorknob.

"What about Joseph?" Her father's normally robust voice was muted.

Rebekah could feel her eyes sparkling as she tipped her face back to her Pa. "He told me he loved me, Pa, even when he knew I was English!"

"What did you say?"

Her surge of enthusiasm ebbed at the presentation of this question. "Oh Pa, I told him I couldn't love him if I didn't love myself, and that I wasn't even sure of who I was. Then, when I turned, he was gone."

Her mother's voice was hushed. "Do you still feel that way, child?"

"No, Ma, I don't."

Elnora studied her daughter. "How do you feel now?"

A grin parted Rebekah's lips. "I love him, Ma. I always have. I always will."

"Then perhaps you should go tell him," Samuel suggested. "No doubt those words stung, and as you now know, it hurts you when you hurt those you love."

She nodded thoughtfully. "Perhaps I'll take him a cinnamon cake. That is his favorite, you know." She kept her tone light and tried to mask the worry she felt deep in her stomach.

What if he's moved on? Or decided his feelings weren't as true as he'd hoped?

With expert hands, Rebekah mixed the ingredients for her favorite cake. She'd made this particular recipe so often that she knew the measurements by heart and could pour them precisely by hand without the aid of a measuring device.

"Put yours in to bake first, Rebekah." Elnora set the plate of cinnamon rolls on the counter. "I'll mix the icing for these in the meantime."

Rebekah slid the pan into the oven. "Thank you, Ma. I'll go change and be right back."

Taking the stairs two at a time, Rebekah's heart galloped in her chest as she rummaged through her sparse selection of dresses.

Hurry, Rebekah. Hurry and go promise your love to Joseph.

She chose a plain black dress and tossed her slightly grubby green one against the wall. Once dressed, she fastened the matching cape about her shoulders. "I'd better get a fresh covering, too."

With a gentle fling, her dingy covering joined her dirty dress on the floor. Rebekah gathered her dirty clothing and made a run through each of the rooms, adding dirty clothes to her pile. A covering lay on the bed in her parent's room and a pair of britches had been shoved into the far corner in the older boys' room. Then, in the little boys' room, she hit the mother lode. Socks were scattered beneath the beds and shirts were wadded under the covers.

Rebekah let the grin grow until she felt the ache in her cheeks. "I love you, boys."

She gathered the little articles and stacked them on her arm. Outside her quilting room, she dropped the laundry into the large, metal washtub that sat in the cubby.

Rebekah dashed down the stairs and was met with the

intoxicating scent of baking cinnamon from the kitchen.

"Just in time." Elnora pulled the fluffy cake from the oven. "Now, in go my cinnamon rolls."

"Thank you, Ma." Rebekah stepped to admire her cake.

Joseph doesn't care much for frosting, so I'll leave it dry. I like it better that way, too.

Her mother held out a square of cheesecloth. "Won't you take it to him now?" Her eyes sparkled beneath her black covering. "The sooner the better, I always say."

Butterflies flitted in her stomach as she accepted the cheesecloth and draped it over the cake. "Oh, Ma, it's still too warm to carry."

Elnora pulled open the drawer. "Here." She extended two thick pads to her. "I made these after your father burnt the other ones by leaving them on the stove."

She could almost hear her heartbeat in her ears as she accepted them. Scooping up her cake, she stepped out the door Elnora already held open. "God's will be done, child," she whispered. "Gelassenheit."

The trek to the Grabers' homestead took much longer than she remembered. Then again, she didn't make the journey much because it seemed Joseph always came to her.

I wonder if he was this nervous when he came to pick me up for the festival. No wonder he looked so out of sorts when he arrived.

Things were so much clearer now. Rebekah wished she could have accepted the truth of her past without having to put everyone she loved through all this rigmarole.

Finally, the Graber homestead came into view. A quietness hung over the place that Rebekah could almost feel. She shuddered. That certainly wasn't a familiar feeling.

Taking each step carefully so as not to damage her cake, Rebekah was surprised when the front door opened before she even knocked.

Lucas stood there, his lips drawn into a thin line. His wide blue eyes, the ones that always seem to be dancing with some untold joke or josh, were subdued. "Hallo, Rebekah."

She bit her lower lip. "Hallo, Mr. Graber. Is Joseph here?"

Lucas shook his head infinitesimally. "He came by for a moment and told us about Peter. Then he left. I've not seen my boy since."

He folded his arms and leaned against the doorway.

A hot knot rose into Rebekah's throat. It seemed hard to breathe. Heat crept into her cheeks and the fluffy cake suddenly seemed awkward and unnecessary.

"Can I, um, *may* I, leave this for when he gets—er, for when Joseph gets…comes home?" She couldn't meet Mr. Graber's eyes.

"Sure."

"Thank you."

Mr. Graber nodded as he took it from her without fanfare.

An odd feeling of being unwelcome pushed Rebekah down the stairs and out onto the path. She turned and started toward home but turned back. With her mouth open as if to speak, she stared back at Mr. Graber.

Her cake now sat at his feet. Still, he leaned against the doorframe on his porch. He nodded.

She closed her mouth and began the long walk home.

CHAPTER ELEVEN

Rebekah clutched her cape around her as she ascended the stairs onto her front porch. The wind had turned chilly and fluffy white clouds that had bloomed in the east grew dark.

Elnora and Sarah Wagler were visiting in the sitting room when she walked in.

Sarah rose and strode across the floor, her arms wide. Rebekah hugged her.

Sarah pulled back and held her at arm's length. "We've decided to have a Bible study here this Wednesday. Your Ma and I decided everyone could bring a dish and we could make an evening of it. Will you make one of your delicious cinnamon cakes?"

She nodded. "I would be honored, thank you."

"Good." With a hearty pat on the arm, Sarah retreated to her seat. "Now, Elnora, we have lots of planning to do."

The old friends huddled together, their companionship easy and natural, as Beanie squeaked from the cradle.

Too antsy to sit still or be cooped in the house, Rebekah climbed the stairs.

What to do? What to do?

Her room was tidy, her quilt was finished, and she wasn't keen to start another yet. Worried thoughts of Joseph flitted about in her mind like moths around a lantern, but she forced them back.

He's fine. Maybe he needed to go off alone like I did.

Rebekah spied the glinting tub of dirty laundry at the end of the hall and skipped to retrieve it. The large bar of lye soap lay on its special shelf, right above the bucket. She plucked it up and dropped it onto the clothes.

"I'm running to the river to get this laundry done, Ma!" Rebekah called as she skipped out the back door.

Sarah's excited voice met her ears instead. "Oh, Elnora, this is going to be the most delicious Bible study of the year. 1888 is a wonderful year for food."

"I should have grabbed a shawl," Rebekah muttered. The wind, unseasonable for March, had grown colder in the few minutes she'd been inside. Something in the breeze smelled frosty, like the winds that blew around Christmastime.

Rebekah quickened her pace to the river. "I'll make short work of this."

She eyed the blackening eastern horizon. Ominous clouds, puffy on the bottom and spiky on the top, hung overhead in a low and threatening manner. She shivered. "At least I have long sleeves."

It had grown so cold so quickly that bits of ice clung to the river bank before being washed downstream by the rushing current.

Ma was right about the weather taking a turn.

Rebekah dumped the clothes in a heap on the bank.

With the lye soap in one hand and her dirty dress in the other, she plunged both into the water. Pricks from the cold stabbed her hands as the current splashed further up her arms than she'd intended. The lower half of her sleeves dripped with river water.

In a hurry, she scrubbed the dirt from her dress before she rinsed it quickly and wrung it out. Satisfied, she laid it out on a flat rock and ignored the bright red hue her hands and arms had taken on. She plucked Abram's dirty socks up and dipped them beneath the water's surface. Skimping on quality, Rebekah wrung them out and placed them on the rock as shivers wracked her frame.

"That will have to be good enough for now," she muttered as her teeth chattered. "I'm going back to the house."

The sound of footsteps on river pebbles caught her attention over the whistling wind.

Joseph!

With the cold momentarily ignored, she turned to embrace the man she loved.

She froze, mid-step, for the curve of the hat wasn't right. It wasn't right at all.

"Hello, Rebekah." If Peter was affected by the impending norther, his voice didn't show it. "Have you had a chance to think about what I told you?"

Her smile softened into a different form as she stepped toward him. "How happy am I to learn that you are a relation." She extended her arms and hugged him tightly. "Thank you for enduring so much to bring me the news." She patted his back and started to release from their embrace.

Peter didn't.

Rebekah squirmed in his grasp. Her heart quickened to a gallop before he finally released her. She stepped back. Her hands were numb and the strings on her covering whipped her face.

His mouth turned downward in a severe frown and tears dripped down his face. He swiped at them with the back of one hand. "Will you return with me to the east?" he called over the howling wind.

"I'm staying here."

Peter cupped a hand around his ear and stepped nearer to her. "What?"

"I'm *staying here*!"

His frown settled into a hard line. "Sister, you've been brainwashed by the plain folk. Once you get to Philadelphia, you'll see how much better off you are. I'm the only family you got." He stepped toward her. "As your older brother, it's my duty to see to your well-being. Now, are you coming with me?"

Despite the wind, Rebekah heard every word. She shook her head. "No, Peter, I'm not."

A note of uncertainty gave her words a scared twang.

"You'll thank me for this someday." Peter pushed up his sleeves. "But if you won't *come* with me, I'll have to *bring* you."

He took a step toward her.

Rebekah glanced around for somewhere to hide. Or

somewhere to run. "No, Peter, it shouldn't be like this."

Fat snowflakes swirled around them and covered the ground in a white sheet.

"I believe she wants to be left alone. It sounds as though she's made up her mind." Joseph's baritone voice drowned the wind out.

Peter whirled, unaware that he'd been snuck up on. "I'm taking her home."

Stepping past him as easily as if he were stepping by the Yoder's pup, Joseph extended his hand to Rebekah. She took it and melted into the warmth of his embrace. "She *is* home."

He kept his back to Peter and spoke into her ear. "Storm's getting worse. Let's go."

The wind wailed and lashed their faces with snowflakes and pieces of sleet. "Let me grab the laundry."

"I'll get it for you," Joseph called. He turned and then turned back to her. "Where is it?"

Rebekah gestured to where she had been sitting only moments before. "It's right—"

Her shout was lost to the wind. The snow had begun to fall so quickly that only the top of the washtub was visible. The laundry and the flat rock were completely blotted out by the mounds of snow.

"It's coming fast." Rebekah heard the trill in her voice as Joseph stepped to retrieve the tub.

"We won't make it to the house." His voice was a shout. "Come on, we have to find shelter."

He pushed the tin bucket into her hands. Filled with snow, it was even heavier than when it was filled with laundry.

"Come on, Peter, we're finding shelter," Rebekah called. Had Joseph not held her arm, she wouldn't have been able to follow him. The conditions had gone from cold to freezing in a moment and the snow didn't appear to have any intention of letting up. She could barely make out Joseph's silhouette in front of her. "Come on, Peter."

Joseph pulled her down to the ground. He gave her a shove from behind, and she found herself in the shelter of a rock cave. A haphazard mess of sticks was piled near the back and it was roomy enough to fit all three of them. Despite the sheltering walls, the air inside was bitterly cold.

Rebekah's hands trembled against the laundry tub and the sleeves of her wet dress were frozen. Not the slushy kind of frozen as her clothing sometimes got while playing outside in the powdery Indiana snow with her brothers. No. Frozen. Stiff. Solid. Into black slabs of ice

Her teeth chattered, and her arms might as well have been chunks of dead wood. She glanced down. The tips of her fingers were as white as though they'd been dipped in candle wax.

Joseph followed her gaze and immediately began rubbing them.

"P-p-p-pete-t-t—" she stuttered. Her tongue felt as frozen as her hands.

So do my eyes. And nose.

"He's not here yet." Joseph cupped his mouth around her hands and blew.

If his breath was warm on her fingers, it went unfelt. "Let's get you warm and then I'll go out after him."

He didn't seem to suffer the effects of the cold nearly as much as her. Then again, he hadn't splashed in the river, either.

"G-g-go n-n-o-o-ow Jo-jo-jo—" Her stutter had worsened, and the chill might well have wrapped itself around her very bones.

"Ssh, don't try to talk." He bent her arms and tucked her fingers under her armpits. "Keep them there, all right?"

Joseph grabbed a handful of sticks from the back of the little cave and broke them into a pile of dry wood. Reaching in one pocket, he produced a little instrument that Rebekah hadn't seen since Rumspringa. Had her mouth not been frozen into a stiff line, she would have smiled at the memory.

"Now, don't tell anyone I have this." He held the wire in one hand and with a quick succession of squeezes, the little rocks at the end of each piece of wire knocked together and produced a spark. Joseph held it down in the middle of the pile of kindling. A moment later, a humble flame appeared. He cocked his mouth into a half-smile. "Now I guess I know why I saved that little flint."

He rubbed his hands up and down Rebekah's arms and situated her closer to the fire. "If it gets low, can you feed it another stick?"

She nodded.

"Good girl. I'm going after your brother. I'll be right back." At the mouth of the little rock cave, he looked back.

I love you. If only her mouth would form the words.

Joseph flashed her that dazzling dimpled smile followed by a wink.

Then, he was gone.

Rebekah focused on the little flame that had grown into a modest fire. Her eyelids drooped, but she would focus on the fire.

It has to be going when the men get back. They'll probably be frozen solid.

Slowly, she removed one hand from under her arm. The feeling was coming back, and her fingers hurt. Badly.

Rebekah ignored the stabbing sensation and tried to wrap her waxy fingers around another stick, but they wouldn't bend. Using her hand like a club, she whacked the wood off the top of the stack.

The pain that shot through her fingers and up her arm was reminiscent of the one winter she'd made the mistake of hopping out of bed barefoot on the cold floor. She'd thought the knifelike stabbing sensations that had shot up her legs then were bad. This was worse.

As the fire caught hold of the new wood, Rebekah held her hands out to soak up as much of the warmth as possible. She whimpered and moaned as the feeling pulsed back into her fingers. Finally, she could bend them, and her mind also relaxed enough to form a coherent thought.

Please, God, protect Joseph and Peter—

Rebekah's prayer was cut short when Joseph fell into the cave. His teeth chattered loudly, and his lips were tinged blue.

"Oh, Joseph, thank God. Come here." She held her arms out to her frosty beau. "Did you find Peter?"

Before he could answer, her brother stumbled in. His hat was gone, and his eyes were wide. They showed more of the whites than the colored part. With blond locks frozen in jumbled swirls, Peter's exposed flesh was red and angry. The whole of his hands and the tip of his nose looked as though they had been dipped in wax, much like Rebekah's fingertips had.

Curling her fingers around three more hunks of wood, Rebekah stoked the fire until it roared in the little rock cavern.

"Th-th-that w-was cl-cl-clos-close." Joseph's words were ragged.

Rebekah stripped his stiff coat off and tossed it beside the fire. "Here, let's get you warm."

He patted her arm with awkward, frozen thumps. "M-melt the s-snow in the t-t-tub for P-P-Peter."

Some of the snow in the tub had already melted, but not all of it. Rebekah slid it as close to the fire as she could without placing it directly in the flames.

His hands shaking, Joseph hurried over next to Peter. "H-hands in the t-tub."

"No." It was obvious Peter wanted nothing to do with Joseph and would certainly not accept help from him.

"Then sit by the f-f-fire, at l-least," Joseph managed.

Pulling his frozen duster over his shoulder, Peter turned to face the mouth of the cave. Rebekah watched his back tremble and shake—he had to be frozen near solid. Foolishly, he refused to accept help.

"Joseph," Rebekah whispered. "Come."

He scooted back to her side.

"Are you all right? How did you find him? We are down to about half of our firewood…" She let her voice trail off as she realized Joseph didn't heed any of her questions or concerns. Instead, he simply stared at her as though seeing her for the first time. The ghost of a smile haunted his lips as he rubbed his hands together near the warmth of the flames. Then again, perhaps it was she who saw him through new eyes.

The spark that passed between them, the freshly proven knowledge that one would always be there for the other, surged through her. In that instant, Rebekah envisioned herself flinging off her covering and running through the woods, the wind in her face and hair blowing free, with only Joseph's hand to guide her. The vision faded to the pair of them kneeling together in their home on a sleepy summer morning, quietly speaking to the Lord together.

In an uncharacteristically bold act, she reached across the small expanse between then and rested her hand on his. Turning his over, he linked his icy fingers through her warm ones, palm to palm.

"I can't feel my hands or feet," Peter announced, mostly to himself.

On instant alert, Rebekah released Joseph's hand and crawled to her brother's side. "Come, let us help you."

He shot her a haughty glare. "Why would you want to help me?"

"Because you're my brother." She tugged on his duster sleeve. "Now please, come."

Peter allowed Rebekah to pull him to the washtub. "I'm not sticking my hands in there."

She glanced at Joseph, who nodded. "You will if you want to keep your fingers and hands."

Joseph helped Rebekah push up Peter's stiff duster sleeves. "Rebekah's right, here. Don't you worry now."

Slowly, they pressed Peter's hands into the water.

"No!"

The man's face contorted in planes that Rebekah had never seen on another's face before. His eyebrows furrowed so closely together, she feared he might rightly explode. With his mouth twisted into a grotesque shape, she could see his teeth fairly well.

"You have the same tooth as I do," she observed absently. Joseph leaned to look.

"She's right." Sure enough, both Peter and Rebekah's right front tooth overlapped the left a little.

Peter's face softened. "I think I'm going to be sick," he managed when he finally maneuvered his mouth back to its regular shape.

Joseph nodded. "We need to warm your nose up, too."

Peter stifled a laugh. "Well, mister, I'm certainly not dipping my head in that bucket there." He shifted his eyes to Rebekah and squirmed on the cold stone floor. "Some here may be tempted to push me all the way in and roast me alive to be rid of me."

Rebekah slipped her covering off and let it fall into the water. From the corner of her eye, she could see Joseph watching her but couldn't judge his reaction. It was custom that an Amish woman not be seen by anyone other than her husband without her covering.

She took a stick and swirled it around in the warm water. "Here, we can use this."

Careful not to make eye contact with either Peter or Joseph, she held out the dripping covering on the stick.

Her brother took one hand out of the water and accepted the stick. "Many thanks." He studied it a moment. "What is this thing anyway?"

Gently, Joseph took the stick. "I'll do it. Your hands need to be in the water."

Peter placed his hands back in the water with only the slightest grimace.

"It's my covering. I've worn one since I was a little girl. All Amish girls do."

Peter rolled his eyes and looked at the piece of fabric Joseph held to his nose. "Why?"

"Tradition, I suppose. Everyone's ma and grandma and sisters and daughters wear them." She shifted on the ground. Having never explained anything of her lifestyle to the English, she chose her words carefully. "We always have and that is simply how it's done."

The man wrinkled his nose, signaling Joseph to remove the cloth. "Traditions stem from somewhere."

Rebekah gazed thoughtfully at him. "The first book of Corinthians explains head coverings. Since women were created last, we cover our heads since we are closer to God." A smile tipped her lips. "Do you understand?"

Peter pulled a hand out of the water and touched the tip of his nose. "I suppose so. Y'all ain't the only one that does that, you know."

Rebekah and Joseph exchanged a look over the crackling fire.

"Catholic folk do, but not all the time. Only in church or Mass."

Joseph held his hands to the fire. "Do you follow that religion?"

"No. I almost did."

Her curiosity piqued. "Almost?"

"Had me a Spanish fiancée and she was Catholic. I attended

Mass with her before she left me." Peter rubbed one hand over his five o'clock shadow before shifting his eyes up to meet hers.

Rebekah's gaze danced to Joseph's, whose eyes sparkled with the same brand of curiosity as hers. "Why did she leave you?"

"I wouldn't become Catholic. Her family wanted me to, though she didn't seem to care if I did or didn't."

Joseph interjected, "Why didn't you convert?"

Peter ducked his head. "All those services were in Spanish or Latin or some dang language. I couldn't understand what they was sayin' one lick."

A gentle laugh rippled through the motley trio. "I wouldn't have converted either," Rebekah said. "Part of knowing God is knowing his Word."

Joseph nodded. "What did you do next, Peter?"

The Englishman's blue eyes sparkled. "You sure you wanna hear all this?"

"Of course. You're my brother." Her lips tilted into an easy smile.

Joseph gestured to the outside. The wind still howled, and the snow had drifted against the mouth of the cave so much that only a miniscule swatch of sky remained visible. "I'll have to clear that out in a while," he said, "But aside from that chore, the three of us have a pretty long while to get to know each other."

CHAPTER TWELVE

They talked long into the night. So long, in fact, that Rebekah didn't realize she'd nodded off until she awoke to find both men asleep, too. Joseph had cleared the mouth of the cave, but now, the coldness of the black night crept in. She shivered.

"Cold?"

Rebekah hugged herself and rocked back and forth. Her gaze flickered to her covering that lay beside the fire. Joseph picked it up.

"Here, I dried it for you." He placed it over her hair, tucking in the blonde wisps that peeked out from under it. Tugging gently on the strings, he centered it. "Feel better?"

He didn't drop his fingers from the strings.

"Much, thank you." She met his eyes, which shone with an inner light. "I love my covering, and I love our way of life."

"Peter seemed interested," he said. "It's a shame he's led such a hard life."

Rebekah's heart grew heavy at the memory of Peter's lament on his hard and lonely life. "It is a shame."

"My prayers were answered when you said you'd stay with us in Gasthof." With his eyes boring into hers, Joseph's calloused thumb brushed her cheek and left a sizzling wake. "I love you, Rebekah."

"Joseph, I—" She glanced at Peter, who was snoring softly.

Her shyness forgotten, Rebekah raised a hand and rested it on Joseph's. He accepted her fingers and squeezed them between his own. "I'm sorry for how I spoke to you. Can you forgive me?"

His voice, soft as down and sweet as honey, came quietly. "I forgave you the moment you said it, and I knew it wasn't true, anyhow."

Joseph's breath, warm on her lips, begged her to lean closer.

Rebekah's hand tightened on his. "I need to tell you, Joseph, I have come to understand myself. I do love who I am—"

With her heart hammering in her chest, she inhaled deeply. Joseph's scent flooded her senses and left her head swimming. "So I can tell you, with an open heart—"

Rebekah paused.

Once this was said, there would be no going back. Things could never be the same between them. The future was uncertain, but the truth cloaked her words and gave her assurance that things would work out for the best. God's will would be done.

Gelassenheit.

"Yes?"

With a directness she'd never practiced before, Rebekah stared into his eyes. "I love you, Joseph Graber. And as you said, I have for as long as I can remember."

The enormity of her words filled the expanse of the little cave. They sat together in the comfortable silence that followed, warmed by spoken truth and shared vows of love.

Can he hear my pounding heart? It sounds like it's echoing to me.

Rebekah didn't pull back as Joseph erased the space between them until her lips were warmed by his moist breath. She closed her eyes. Softly and without words, Joseph sealed the gap between them.

The kiss was over in an instant. *But this moment's effects will last a lifetime.*

"Come here." Joseph's voice was low as he lifted his arm.

She leaned into him. His arm draped easily about her shoulders. She fit there, by his side, with such exactitude that it seemed one had been divinely made for the other. There they sat, snug in the warmth of their shared feelings, and the little cave didn't seem so chilled, after all.

"Storm's over!" Peter announced, and his deep voice echoed off the rocks. The words met Rebekah's sleep-heavy ears. Something covered her. Struggling to focus her bleary eyes, she saw the something was black.

Joseph's jacket.

Her lips turned up in a sleepy smile as she beheld the sight of him curled up with his back to her.

He must be freezing.

She draped the warm jacket carefully over him.

"Good morning, Peter."

His eyebrows arched skyward and a smile stretched his lips wide. "Didn't you hear me? Storms over!" He gestured wildly to the door. "We can get out of here."

And visit an outhouse.

Peter reached over and gave Joseph's shoulder a shake. "Hey, Joseph. Hey there. Come on, wake up. Let's get out of here."

Joseph sat up. With a dimpled smile and squinted eyes, he rubbed his inky curls. "That's good news, Peter."

Rebekah watched as he stretched and tried to shake the sleep from his brain. He linked his fingers and arched forward, his arms extended before him. Mid-stretch, he glanced at her.

Heat flooded her cheeks.

"Good morning, Rebekah." The gleam in his eye hinted at some secret only the two of them shared. "Ready to go home?"

The scarlet cooled as quickly as it flared. "Yes!"

A loud rumble from her stomach sent an easy chuckle through the lot of them.

"Then let's go."

Outside, the deep gray sky was thick with low-lying clouds. To the east, bright and clear blue sky hinted at the truth in Peter's words. Indeed, the unexpected storm was over.

"See, it's over." Peter flung his arms over his head. "Snow's deep, though."

Peter and Joseph had cleared the snow from the mouth of the cave overnight, so the area outside was relatively clear. Rebekah shifted her weight on her already icy feet.

"Let's go."

Trudging off in the direction of the Stoll home, Joseph led the way and scooped at the waist-deep snow with Rebekah's washtub. "If that storm had lasted any longer," he huffed, "We would have been in real trouble."

Rebekah stepped close behind him.

"I'll take over when you get tired, Joseph," Peter offered from behind her.

Joseph nodded, his wide-brimmed black hat a stark contrast to the ocean of surrounding snow.

After only a short distance, Rebekah tugged at her cape and her teeth chattered.

This is going to be a long walk, God, please help us make it home.

Heaviness weighted her shoulders.

"Here, sister, you look cold." Peter's thick duster was warm about her shoulders. "Here, Joseph, my turn." He slipped past Rebekah, retrieved the washtub, and commenced flinging snow.

Joseph took his place behind Rebekah, his angular face red. "Snow's heavy," he breathed.

"Hey!" Peter gestured ahead. "There are men." He flung the snow with a newfound ferocity. "It's your people. Over here!"

"Over here, over here!" chorused Rebekah and Joseph. Her tender fingers burned from the cold. She tucked them deep in the duster pockets.

A chattering of German and English filled the chilled, soupy air as the familiar voices of Mr. Graber, Mr. Yoder, Mr. Wagler, and Mr. Knepp met their ears.

"I see someone!"

"Get the buggy!"

Rebekah quickened her steps to keep up with Peter, who took off at a trot.

Above all, Samuel's voice rode the wind. "My daughter, is she there?"

Her words tore from her throat in a scream as Joseph waved his hat high above them. "I'm here, Pa!"

Samuel's new draft horses marched easily through the snow.

They even seemed to enjoy it, swishing their tails and stepping lively.

Thank you, God.

"Thank God, they're alive!" Lucas Graber's voice bounced along the snow. "Come, get in the buggy!"

The snow made the buggy ride rough, but the draft horses didn't seem to mind.

"The storm came out of nowhere while I was doing laundry, Pa." Rebekah leaned against her Pa. "The clothes are still there." An apologetic note hung on her words. "Somewhere."

"Clothes are replaceable, Rebekah. You aren't." Holding her tightly beneath his arm, he glanced at Joseph. "Are you to thank for saving my little girl?"

Lucas snapped the reins. "Always in the right place at the right time, aren't you, son?"

Joseph did a half smile. "Well, in part. Peter here helped, too."

Samuel nodded at Peter.

"Well," he whispered to Rebekah. "Your ma is worried something horrible. Everyone's at the house. We've been looking for you since the snow stopped."

Snuggling deep against her pa, she allowed herself to doze the rest of the ride home.

CHAPTER THIRTEEN

Indeed, every family in Gasthof Village was at the Stolls. The women circled in the sitting room, Bibles open, as the Yoder pup bounced from person to person.

Tears streamed from Elnora's eyes as she rushed to greet them. "My baby!" She wrapped Rebekah in a tight embrace. "Thank God!"

"It *was* God, Ma. Everything about this has been by His hand." She gestured to Joseph and Peter as they climbed the steps in unison. "He made sure they were there. We all needed each other to survive."

Elnora waved her arm to include all of them. "Come in, all of you, and warm yourselves by the fire." Baby Beanie squeaked from his cradle. "We were about to have a church service. Her broad face beamed. "Peter, won't you join us?"

"Thank you kindly, ma'am. That's a mighty kind offer, considering all I've put you folks through. My apologies." He tipped his hat to Elnora. "But I'd best be goin'."

Rebekah's heart sank. The moment had been so perfect, it hadn't even occurred to her that he would leave. She'd assumed he'd stay, though she hadn't really given the matter much thought aside from her rapid assumption.

Peter extended his hand to Joseph, who accepted it and shook with three brisk shakes. "Many thanks for saving my fingers.

Surely, they wouldn't be here if it weren't for you making me stick them in that awful water." He grinned and twitched his nose. "And my smeller, too."

Dropping his voice low, he continued. "No one's ever done anything so kind. I wasn't expecting that kindness, especially after I was so horrible to you."

"God commands us to love and forgive each other, Peter. Like He loves and forgives us."

Peter looked genuinely puzzled. "That must have been what they said when they were speakin' Latin. Don't recall that."

Rebekah smiled. "It says so right in the Lord's Prayer. *Forgive us our trespasses as we forgive those who trespass against us.*"

Her brother broke from his handshake with Joseph. "Mr. Stoll, if I could collect my wagon, I'll be on my way." He jammed his hat on his head with a nod to Rebekah. "Goodbye Hannah-Rebekah Stoll." A grin broke his stoic face into an array of happy creases.

Remembering his duster, which was still around her shoulders, she followed him. "Wait, Peter!" She unwound the coat and held it out to him. "Thank you for finding me."

He brushed the top of her covering with a light kiss. "Thank you for being you."

He slipped his arms in the duster and descended the stairs without looking back.

In the warmth of her childhood home, surrounded by the people she loved, Rebekah searched her heart to the backdrop of Mr. Graber reading from the book of Ecclesiastes, for the reason her smile seemed forced.

Joseph sat closer than usual on her father's hand-hewn loveseat. Normally, that would be cause for her heart to soar and her smile to stay plastered across her lips for days. As she glanced from face to familiar face, a rogue tear escaped and slid dramatically down her cheek.

Joseph bumped her with his elbow. "Are you ill?"

She bit her lip to keep the flood of sudden emotion at bay and nodded. She slammed her eyes shut in a desperate attempt to keep the wall of tears from spilling over. "I miss my brother."

A series of sharp knocks on the front door brought Mr. Graber's sermon to a halt. "A day of surprises."

Lucas opened the door.

Tears cascaded down Rebekah's cheeks in a shimmering veil. She stood slowly.

There, with a tear-streaked face and the tip of his nose red as a holly berry, stood Peter.

"I couldn't leave." His tears began afresh. "I don't have a soul in the world. Nobody except you." His eyes locked with hers.

Sobbing, she dashed across the room and into his waiting arms. There, she wept in harmony with her newest—and finally older—brother. "I'm so glad you came back."

"Me too, sister."

Samuel Stoll cleared his throat. "Peter?"

Releasing Rebekah, he swiped at his eyes with the back of one hand. "Mr. Stoll, I'm sure there's rules about stuff like this, but—" He flickered his watery gaze around the room at each of the faces that stared back at him. "If it sounds fittin' to you, I'd like to stay on. I'm handy with steel and can make some of the strongest horseshoes north of the Mason-Dixon."

From the corner of her eye, Rebekah saw him suck in his lower lip.

Just like me.

"I know that took courage, Peter," Samuel said cautiously, "but you're right. Things like this aren't normally done."

Mr. Graber coughed. "Perhaps we could call a meeting of the elders and discuss the matter further?"

Mr. Yoder rose slowly, following Mr. Raber, Mr. Graber, Mr. Knepp, and Mr. Wagler into the Stoll kitchen. With a fleeting glance at Elnora, Samuel fell into step behind Mr. Odon and pulled the door shut after them.

"I reckon they'll decide, then?" Peter's voice broke the uneasy silence that had befallen the room. "I mean, if I can stay?"

Elnora plucked Beanie from his cradle and nestled him to her chest. The quilt Rebekah had given him as his very first gift was wrapped securely around him. "Tell me, Peter, do you love God?"

The women of Gasthof Village stared at him with stoic faces. Even bubbly Annie Knepp sat silent and still beside Katie.

Twisting his hat in circles before him, Peter looked at Joseph, who gave him an encouraging nod. "We were church goin' folk before my parents died. I kind of lost my way after that." He gestured to Rebekah. "As I was telling Hann—Rebekah—and Joseph last night, I attended Catholic Masses before."

Elnora smiled. "That's fine and good, but do you *love the Lord*."

"I ain't never professed it outright, but I got to see a little of His love since I found you folks. I could get mighty used to it."

Mrs. Odom, perhaps the quietest woman in the settlement, spoke in her soft, singsong voice. "If you would like to receive our Lord as your savior, all you have to do is ask Him, Peter."

"It's as easy as all that?"

Annie and Katie's mother answered. "It is. But in doing that, you've promised to live your life for Him and His Glory."

Peter nodded. "That makes the most sense of anything I've heard in a while." He eased down into an open spot on the floor. "All them churches I visited made it seem a whole lot more difficult."

The Yoder pup bounded into his lap, his pink tongue flying on its own with reckless abandon.

Heloise adjusted her splinted leg. "It can be difficult, but if you're sincere in asking for His forgiveness and turning from sin, He will give it."

"Like I told you earlier," Joseph added, "Love and forgive others as He loves and forgives us. That's the main rule right there."

Rebekah's pulse quickened at Peter's enthusiasm and that of her family and friends to answer his questions. "Attend church meetings and do good works by helping your neighbors to show His love. That's our way of life."

Before Peter could answer, the kitchen door squeaked open. The elder men of Gasthof Village emerged. Their expressionless faces revealed nothing of a decision or lack thereof.

Samuel Stoll stepped forward. "Peter?"

He rose, hat in hand. "Yessir?"

"Come stand here before us."

Peter did as he was commanded with his blue eyes as wide as a child's.

Samuel cleared his throat. "Your only relation is Rebekah, and you wish to join our community here in Gasthof Village, correct?"

Peter bobbed his head.

"Your intention is to join our Amish community. To live as us, dress as us, work as us, to love God, work for Him every day, and in turn, be a member of our church and society?"

Peter puffed his chest out. "Yessir, that is correct." His sure words echoed off the walls of the house.

Samuel glanced back at the other elders. "Very well. We have come to a decision."

"Sir, may I say one thing before you tell me your decision?"

Rebekah sucked in her breath and shared a glance with Joseph. He appeared as eager to hear the decision as her. All the good-natured chatter had ceased when the men reemerged, and an almost tangible tension hung in the air.

Just let Pa tell us yes or no!

"I understand if the decision is no, I see why you want to keep your ways on the straight and narrow. It's a mean world out there. I've lived it, I know." Peter glanced at the faces of the women. "But since meeting you all, my life's already changed for the better. I can only imagine, if given the chance to become a part of you, a part of your faith, a part of your traditions…" He shook his head. "Well, that'd be almost heaven."

A few of the women bounced a knowing smile between them.

Peter continued. "Despite what your decision is today, it's important for me to tell you I've changed. Even if I leave here alone today, your family has changed my life for the better, and for that I'm forever indebted to you."

Samuel crossed his arms. "One year."

"Sir?"

"Live with us, as we do, for one year." Samuel glanced at the faces of his friends and family. "If, on this day next year, you still wish to join us, you may."

Rebekah's knees quaked, and happiness bubbled in her stomach. Unable to contain herself, she clapped her hands together in a sharp snap. Joseph laughed.

Simon Wagler stepped forward, his hand outstretched. "I'm

Simon Wagler. It was my son, Elijah, who pointed you here in the first place."

Peter's eyes widened as he grasped Mr. Wagler's hand.

"That there's my wife, Sarah." He nodded toward the throng of women. "We'd be much obliged if you'd stay with us for the duration of this year."

"Thank you, Mr. Wagler. I'd be much obliged." Peter's smile was so wide that it seemed he could hardly force his mouth to form words.

Simon clapped Peter on the back. "Come on then, let's get you into some more fitting attire."

"Ma, can we come down now? Jeremiah's read our Bible lesson to us *four times* already." Thomas's tiny voice sounded supremely put-out. Glancing down the stairs, his eyes lit on Rebekah. "Sissy!"

Quicker than a fish could find a hole in a fishing net, Thomas flew down the stairs and into Rebekah's waiting arms. The rest of the Stoll boys thundered after him. "Sissy. Oh sissy, you're alive! I prayed for you all night long." Wrapping his little arms around her neck, he buried his face in her shoulder. His tiny hat fell to the floor.

"I love you, littlest brother."

Thomas sniffled. "I love you, too."

In the midst of the commotion, Rebekah noticed Joseph and her father slip out the front door.

Probably getting something for Peter or putting up his wagon.

Well-wishes from the Stoll boys ended with Jeremiah approaching Rebekah last. "I didn't like your display at breakfast the other day."

"I'm really sorry, Jeremiah. I meant to apologize to you and the boys when I got home, but everyone was fishing, and I went to wash the clothes—"

He held up his thirteen-year-old hand. "But I probably would have made an even bigger scene if I'd had gotten the same news." He grinned. "Welcome home."

She grasped her biggest little brother in a tight embrace and planted a kiss on the top of his best hat. "Thank you, I missed you."

Jeremiah flushed and waved her off. He turned toward the

kitchen, where Heloise Graber had started serving the lunch. Before he stepped away, he turned back. "Missed you, too."

"Rebekah?" Her pa's voice called her attention away from the little men. "Joseph asked me to tell you that he's on the front porch if you need to find him."

"Did he wish to speak with me, Pa?" She glanced from side to side. "Pa?"

Hmm, where'd he go?

Rebekah wove through the families of Gasthof Village until she finally arrived at the front door.

"Rebekah?" Katie's voice came from beside her.

"Hallo, Katie." She placed her hand on the doorknob. "I finished my quilt, thanks to your squares."

"Good. Um, Rebekah, I was wondering…"

"Yes?"

The girl stared at her hands. "If, well, the next time you talk to Peter—" Her gaze danced around Rebekah. "If you might tell him I know a great place to picnic."

Katie spun on her heels and retreated into the mass of people. Rebekah's jaw went slack as she watched her.

Is her neck flushed? Oh my, Katie is blushing!

An invisible weight lifted as Rebekah slipped her cloak about her shoulders and stepped out to join Joseph on the porch.

"I'm glad you came out." He stepped toward her. "It's still below freezing out here, so this won't take long." His lips quivered, and his hands were deep in his pockets.

Rebekah danced from foot to foot. Indeed, it was frosty out. She cupped her hands and blew on her already-throbbing fingers. "Is everything all right?"

"Everything's more than all right, Rebekah." Drawing ever nearer, he took one hand from his pocket. Letting it brush the side of her face, he remained silent while the little puffs from their breath in the frozen air mingled between them.

Icy fingers grasped her stomach and sent a rush of nervous butterflies fluttering through her body. "Katie stopped me on the way out—"

Joseph laid a finger lightly on her lips. "I don't want to talk about Katie. I want to talk about you. And us."

With her knees threatening to give way, Rebekah dropped her

voice to a whisper. "I don't really want to talk about Katie either, even if she may be my sister-in-law someday."

His eyes glimmered as he stared into hers. "Maybe she'll be mine, too."

Rebekah paused as the weight of his words met her heart. "Yours...*too*?"

"There was one thing we didn't talk about after the festival the other day." Sinking down until he was balanced before her on one knee, Joseph drew the other hand out of his pocket. "My one regret from Rumspringa."

"What regret?"

"For not doing this." On the end of Joseph's finger glittered a thin band of gold. "It was my grandma's. She left it to me in hopes I would give it to my future wife. May I see your hand?"

Rebekah lowered her hand into his.

Dreaming. I'm dreaming. I must be dreaming.

"Rebekah Elnora Stoll," he began as he slipped the delicate ring on the appropriate finger. "Will you join with me in creating a future?"

"Oh, Joseph." Her words came out in a squeak. She sank to her knees and grasped both of his hands in hers. "Yes. Yes, I will marry you!"

Slipping one hand behind her neck, Joseph pulled her close. His lips brushed hers as he spoke. "I love you, Rebekah, now and forever."

She closed her eyes. "I love you, Joseph. You and no other. Forever."

His cold fingertips on her neck sent shivers down her spine as their lips met, sealing the promise of their eternal love and devotion as the snowflakes began to fall again.

Joseph rose and helped Rebekah to her feet. Already, fresh snow swirled around them. He extended his hand. "Ready to go tell the families?"

She took his hand and twined her fingers through his. "Ready."

Joseph placed his hand on the doorknob and turned his face toward her. "Well, Miss Stoll, are you ready to start the next part of our lives together?"

He winked, and her stomach twisted in knots.

"I'm ready, Mr. Graber. Let's do it." She exhaled the breath she didn't even realize she'd been holding. "Together."

MEET THE AUTHOR

Sara Harris is a native west Texan, conservationist, certified teacher, and certifiable Gypsy. Sara and family have made their hope in places all over the world, from the majestic Oklahoma plains to the eclectic mountains of Italy – collecting inspiration and rescue animals along the way.

Sara is married to a man who makes romance novel heroes pale in comparison and, with him, manages their tribe of children and pets. She has her Bachelor of Arts degree in Medieval European History and is a member of the Romance Writers of America, Hearts Through History, Western Fictioneers, West Houston Romance Writers. She is represented by Julie Gwinn of The Seymour Literary Agency. Keep up with her at www.saraharrisbooks.com.

ACKNOWLEDGEMENTS

Thank you to my beautiful children – it was your experiences and adventures that inspired this book and these characters (especially the mischievous, bread-swiping, rooster-wrangling boys). You guys always support Mom's writing and in turn have blossomed into authors yourselves! You make me so proud, all six of you.

Thank you to my wonderful husband, Wesley. Romance novel heroes pale in comparison to you. Thank you for your unending love and support…and for keeping me full of coffee. But most of all, thank you for choosing me as your heroine to do this life with.

Thank you to my amazing agent, Julie Gwinn of The Seymour Agency. Thank you for your excitement over this and all my projects, your tenacity, your know-how, and most of all, thank you for being my agent!

Thank you to Dawn at Vinspire Publishing for falling in love with Joseph and Rebekah and for allowing their tale to be told.

Thank you to each of you readers! I pray Rebekah and Joseph's adventures, heartaches, and heartbreaks help you deepen your relationship with God and strengthen your faith. Happy reading!

Dear Reader,

If you enjoyed reading *Rebekah's Quilt*, I would appreciate it if you would help others enjoy this book, too. Here are some of the ways you can help spread the word:

Lend it. This book is lending enabled so please share it with a friend.

Recommend it. Help other readers find this book by recommending it to friends, readers' groups, book clubs, and discussion forums.

Share it. Let other readers know you've read the book by positing a note to your social media account and/or your Goodreads account.

Review it. Please tell others why you liked this book by reviewing it on your favorite ebook site.

Everything you do to help others learn about my book is greatly appreciated!

Sara Harris

PLAN YOUR NEXT ESCAPE!
WHAT'S YOUR READING PLEASURE?

Whether it's captivating historical romance, intriguing mysteries, young adult romance, illustrated children's books, or uplifting love stories, Vinspire Publishing has the adventure for you!

For a complete listing of books available, visit our website at www.vinspirepublishing.com.

Like us on Facebook at www.facebook.com/VinspirePublishing

Follow us on Twitter at www.twitter.com/vinspire2004

Follow our blog for details of our upcoming releases, giveaways, author insights, and more! www.vinspirepublishingblog.com.

We are your travel guide to your next adventure

CPSIA information can be obtained
at www.ICGtesting.com
Printed in the USA
BVHW031039221221
624595BV00011B/1564

9 781732 711259